GREED W̶A̶S̶ ̶P̶R̶E̶C̶I̶OUS

TRUST WAS EXTINCT!

I looked away into a dim corner as if catching sight of something alarming. The moment their eyes turned with mine I squeezed the trigger and let go with a burst right at the armed men. Then I ran like hell out of the room and down the hall and the marble steps and into the courtyard to the van, bullets flying everywhere. I started the motor, my foot pushing the pedal to the floor, and took off, careening out of the Palazzo past the guards at the gate and through a furious fusillade drumming on the sides. Out into the empty black street, not knowing where to go. Driving crazily, feverishly, all the time wondering if Scala had set me up. . .

We will send you a free catalog on request. Any titles not in your local book store can be purchased by mail. Send the price of the book plus 50¢ shipping charge to Tower Books, P.O. Box 270, Norwalk, Connecticut 06853.

Titles currently in print are available for industrial and sales promotion at reduced rates. Address inquiries to Tower Publications, Inc., Two Park Avenue, New York, New York 10016, Attention: Premium Sales Department.

MUSSOLINI'S GOLD

John Kimmey

TOWER BOOKS NEW YORK CITY

All wars are boyish, and are fought by boys.

—Herman Melville

A TOWER BOOK

Published by

Tower Publications, Inc.
Two Park Avenue
New York, N.Y. 10016

Copyright © 1981 by John Kimmey

Printed in the United States

Chapter 1

Florence signed off at six-twenty, and I quickly decoded the message on the one-time pad: "Ben and gold leave Milan tonight for Valtellina. Seize and hold at Como for 1st Div. Corvo." Without bothering to write the words on a piece of paper, I ripped off the tissuelike sheets and raced out of the radio room to find the major.

The villa was quiet. Only the wind off the lake and the rain broke the silence. The hall felt cold and eerie like all the twenty-two rooms abandoned since the beginning of the war.

Midway down the stairs the captain stood blocking my path—the bushy mustache, the paratroop boots, the .45 on his web belt. Stocky and dark-haired, he looked grim in the faint light from the overhead bulb.

"What is it, Vic?"

"Message from Corvo for the major."

"Hand it here." He moved up a couple of steps.

"He wanted me to give it to him personally."

"He's not feeling well. He's gone to bed."

"To bed?" I glanced down the hall toward his room. "I didn't hear him come up."

"You were transmitting. He got sick at supper."

"You guys sending him to Switzerland without shoes?" I stared down at the swarthy figure staring up at me.

"Why would we do that?"

"You want to take over and order more arms drops

for your Commie friends."

"You on his side?"

"I'm on nobody's side. I'm just the operator on this mission."

"You're going to have to choose now, though. Things are changing around here. How about it? Let's have the message." He took another step up, a slight smile playing around his small mouth.

"I can't. He said if anything came in he had to see it first no matter what." I started to turn down the hall toward the major's room. The dim bulb flickered as if about to go out and plunge the hall into darkness. Below, voices echoed through the hollow rooms.

"Don't bother him. He's too sick to know what's going on. I'm second in command, remember."

"This is urgent."

"A new drop?"

"The end of the war."

"Jesus, let's have it then, Sergeant." He reached the landing and stood a couple of feet away. His black eyes bore into me. "Hell, if it's about over, we've got to get out of here fast and head for Milan. That's our main job, to work with the CLNAI before the Fifth Army arrives in the city. Liaison with the partisan command. We can't stay here in this godforsaken place."

"I thought your job was building a Red army up here. Don't you guys want to take over the country by V-E Day?"

"That's none of your damn business," he snapped. "Just give me that message. It's my show now. I'm the one who's giving orders." He reached out to grab me. I jerked back. He unholstered the .45 and for a second I froze, watching his right hand go to the stock. Then I turned and strode down the hall.

"Sergeant!" he roared. I kept on going, waiting for the shot.

The high-ceilinged blue room was dusky, only one weak bulb shedding any light. The major lay on the mattress of the canopied bed dressed in OD's, the shirt

6

open at the collar, paratroop boots unlaced, gasping, gray-looking. A tall heavy man with rugged features, he always reminded me of an outdoorsman, though in civilian life he was a Wall Street lawyer. Once he confessed in confidence that General Donovan had asked him to head the mission in order to keep an eye on D'Alessandro and the two OG lieutenants with him, Bruno and Carlo. They had all fought in the Spanish Civil War together and were in contact with Togliatti and the Italian Communist Party. Although I sympathized with them and their support of the Garibaldi brigades and was against his favoring the Christian Democrats and the Catholic Action Party in ordering drops, I did feel sorry for the poor guy up here all alone against these pros. They held him in contempt for his capitalistic background and his ignorance of guerrilla warfare. Besides, he knew little of the country and couldn't speak the language. Typical of so many OSS officers sent on special missions behind the lines because they were friends of the general. One night parachuting into Corsica and two weeks later back dancing at the Waldorf Astoria. Only now MacGregor didn't look as if he'd ever see New York again.

"The captain says you're not feeling too well, sir." I stood over him. His brown eyes focused on me. The gray streaks in his hair seemed to be turning white almost before my eyes. His body shook in spasms as he coughed and retched.

"I think there was something in my soup tonight, Vic," he said in a hoarse whisper.

"You mean they poisoned you?"

"I don't know. But I don't think I'm going to make it out of here." His eyelids looked heavy, his face sagged, his tall frame seemed shrunken.

"You got a message from Corvo. Mussolini's headed for Como with the whole Fascist treasury. We're supposed to seize him."

"We don't have the men for that. I can't—" His voice faded out.

7

"Want me to give the message to the captain?"

"He probably knew it was coming. That's why—What's today?"

"Tuesday, April 24."

"Didn't the Fifth Army break through the Gothic Line at Bologna a couple of days ago?"

"That's what I picked up from the BBC."

"See if you can get in contact with Florence. I don't trust D'Alessandro. He's planning something, he and those damn Reds. Bill warned me about him." He paused and coughed. "But I never thought he'd go this far. We're still in the army up here. I'm still in command. We had our disagreements about drop priorities, but—" He lost his voice again. It was like a signal fading in a bunch of static. I watched him, waiting for the death rattle to start. "Do your best. Don't let them. . ."

He grimaced as he spoke, writhed, choked, became inarticulate. I stood gazing down at the helpless old man not knowing what the hell to do, smelling the vomit caked on his shirt, the yellow stuff drooling out of his mouth, seeing the pain creasing his face. He kept trembling and growing paler and paler. I started for the door to call downstairs.

The captain marched in with Carlo and Bruno, one short and squat, the other taller and thinner. Behind them were two twenty-year-old partisans, Giorgio and Salvatore from the Second Garibaldi Brigade in the Vall d'Ossola region. They wore red metal stars on their lapels and tricolored neckerchiefs and carried Sten guns. And to think when I first saw them a month ago they appeared so picturesque with their Alpine hats topped with an eagle feather.

"You guys come to put him out of his misery?" I faced the five of them lined up at the foot of the bed. D'Alessandro had his .45 out.

"We just got word the Krauts are planning to attack the villa. We've got to beat it out of here by midnight. And we can't take him with us. He's too damn sick.

And we can't take a chance of them seizing him either and making him talk. It'd blow the whole mission, jeopardize all our people in the area."

"Why not take him to a doctor? There must be one around."

"He'd be too scared of reprisals to treat him. And somebody would inform on him. No, he's got to go, Sergeant. Sorry, there's no other way. Too much is at stake."

He strode forward and brushed me aside to stand over the major, the .45 raised above the body on the bed shaking worse than ever, sweat breaking out over his face. His eyes bulged as he gazed up at the captain and then at me now on the other side of him. He tried to raise his hands to push away the gun. He tried to speak. Only his lips moved.

"Say a prayer for him, will you?" D'Alessandro glanced over at me. I mumbled something half outloud, pondering a dark corner of the room. The others at the foot of the bed stood impassive, watching with a kind of fascinated curiosity as if they were interns witnessing an operation.

He pulled the trigger, once, twice. The sounds in the room made one terrific explosion. The body jerked a couple of times and lay still. Blood soaked the mattress and dripped to the floor. Flesh and bone splattered against the walls. There wasn't much left of his head except for a shredded red mass above the neck.

"Now how about that message, Sergeant?" he looked over at me. "It concerned Il Duce and the gold, didn't it?"

I handed him the wet sheets crumpled up in my fist, nauseous, still not able to gaze fully at the corpse practically headless on the bed. After studying the onion skin sheets for a couple of minutes, he thrust them in his pocket.

"So I was right, wasn't I? Okay, we head for Como to pick up the big bastard and all the marbles. Ready, you guys?" The men at the foot of the bed nodded and smiled.

"What are you going to do with me?"

"You're coming along. What else? We need that radio."

"Then what?"

"That all depends on how well you play follow the leader."

"How are you going to explain this?"

"We'll take care of it, don't worry. I'll give you a message to send to Florence before we leave. Better go down now and eat some supper. You've got a long night ahead of you."

I didn't move.

"Don't worry. You won't get food poisoning. He just ate a green apple, that's all. And don't try to run off. You'll never make it. There are too many guys out there just waiting to take pot shots at you."

"The Fifth Army will be here soon."

"Not for a couple of days. A lot can happen in a short time. So be a good boy and do what we tell you and you'll go home to momma."

My eyes fell to the pools of fresh blood and bits of flesh and bone on the mattress and floor.

"That's the right spirit, Vic. Don't worry. Everything's going to come out all right. The major had to go one way or another. It was in the cards from the beginning. If he had been a little more cooperative, things might have gone easier for him. You just remember that."

I walked back to my room and the SSTR-1 on the table, thinking about raising Florence on the Guard Channel and sending a message in the clear. Instead I sat on the bed wondering what to do next. Obviously they had to get rid of me in order to make their story about the major's death stick. Still that wouldn't be for a while, not as long as I had the radio and they needed contact with headquarters. So the best thing was to wait and take my chances and when the opportunity arose make a break for it. Get my revenge on the sons-ofbitches too. MacGregor wasn't any father figure. I didn't like his politics or his autocratic manner. He always acted somehow as if he were above us. But then I thought of my old man and felt the pieties surging through me, the drums for revenge beating harder and harder. Christ, I wanted to make them pay for his death!

The five of them marched by in the hall carrying the body wrapped in an army blanket stained with blood. I shuffled after them, down the stairs and through the great shadowy rooms full of guns and drop canisters and boxes of K rations and explosives. They went into the terraced garden and through the gate to the beach below. Stopping at the boathouse dock, they put the body in what looked like a canvas bag. Then the two partisans climbed into a rowboat and Carlo and Bruno set the corpse in front. They loaded on rocks and a coil of rope. I thought about running back to the villa, grabbing a Sten gun and returning to wipe the bastards out as they stood watching the pallbearers drifting away into the rain and the darkness.

Or beating it out of there. I figured I could always go back to the seminary on the island where we hid the first couple of weeks in February after the jump on Mount Mottarone during a rastrellamento. The priests had been good to us and would remember me. And I could stay in that loft high above the sacristy again, living on cheese and wine and rice until the liberation of the area and the Fifth Army arrived. Nobody would think of searching for me there.

They tramped back to the villa past me hiding in the bushes, not saying a word. After a few minutes I went in and confronted them. They were packing—rolling up their sleeping bags, stuffing rations in their packs, taking ammo out of boxes, picking up the guns lying around and loading them.

"You'll never get away with it," I said in the doorway.

"So you saw us down there at the lake, huh, Vic?"

11

D'Alessandro turned on me.

"Yeah, I saw. Giorgio and Salvatore coming back?"

"Oh, sure. Soon as they dump the old man. Then we're heading for Como and hitting the jackpot. You know there's supposed to be half a million in that convoy, kid."

"I thought you guys were Commies, not capitalists. You were up here to liberate oppressed people."

"We are, we are. We're going to capture the big prick and his gold and you're going to help us. But that doesn't mean we can't put a few lire in our pockets while we're doing it. You too. You can help yourself."

"I'm a soldier, not a war profiteer."

"Okay, then, the first thing is to send this message on the Guard Channel." He walked over and handed me a slip of paper: "MacGregor sick. Had to leave me. Germans coming to villa tonight. Off to Como. D'Alessandro."

I studied the words and waited for him to speak.

"Don't add anything. Carlo will go along to make sure you don't. Capeesh, Sergeant?"

I went back up to my room with the little chubby guy following. He examined the one-time pad sheet with the English written under the code letters. Then he sat with me on the bed and waited for Florence to respond to my signal.

After the transmission he left, and I packed the radio in the suitcase and lugged it and my bedroll and carbine downstairs. They were waiting in their panchos by the front door. Giorgio and Salvatore had returned and were grinning away. Although my age they seemed older, tougher, and more experienced somehow. I was sure that they held me in as much contempt as did Bruno and Carlo, who reminded me more of those Mafia type OSS recruited from the Purple Gang in Philadelphia than they did of Spanish Civil War veterans. Ever since the mission began it seemed they had been kidding me about my Ivy League background, Dartmouth '44, and my plans after the war to go to law

12

school.

"Well, Vic, feel any better now?" D'Alessandro said. "That the first man you ever saw die?"

"The first one I ever saw executed, and I hope the last."

"Too cold-blooded for your taste?"

"What the hell do you think?"

"I think, kid, you're finally learning what life is all about behind the lines. It gets pretty complicated sometimes when you don't understand everything that's going on. Now let's get out of here and finish this fuckin' mission. And no funny business. Don't think we'll hesitate to take care of you the way we did the old man if we have to."

We straggled out of the villa and up the dirt road to the highway. It was nine-thirty, cold and rainy, a slight mist falling. No sound of a truck and no sign of any Germans.

"The lorry will be here in a couple of minutes," the captain said. "Just put down your gear and relax. It's a long way to Como. If we're lucky and don't meet any roadblocks or have to make too many detours, we ought to be there by midnight. Let's hope the big Moose arrives in style."

"How are you going to take him?"

"Giorgio and Salvatore have friends in the area. It won't be hard. We'll just stop the convoy somewhere, kidnap the old fart, scoop up the money, and run like hell. The way they do in those Westerns. It should be fun. They say that road up Lake Como on the west side is pretty narrow and made for an ambush. Right, you guys?" He turned to the two partisans standing to one side watching us. They understood English, although they rarely spoke it.

"What do you need a radio for?"

"We've got to keep Florence informed where we are, don't we, tell them what we're doing? And, of course, when we stick up the big bastard, we've got to send word so they can announce it to the world. Jesus, won't

13

that be something. We could have one of the biggest damn celebrations you ever saw. A regular orgy. Kill the son-of-a-bitch and burn his body the way they used to do in the old Roman days. What did they call those things anyway?''

"You mean funeral pyres?" I said.

"Yeah, that's right. Good. You're going to be useful to us, Vic. Education in the service of the masses."

But as they stood there by the side of the road in the darkness, the rain beating down and the woods dripping and the mountains looming across the lake through the mist, they didn't seem like men about to make history or participate in an orgy. The reminded me of a bunch of bad guys out to kill the leader of a rival gang and steal his money.

Chapter 2

We arrived at Como at two A.M. after a long, slow detour north through Varese to escape a Kraut convoy of engineers coming up from the south and heading for Merano and the Brenner Pass. Mussolini, we learned, was still at the Prefecture along with General Graziani. He had been there since nine-thirty and was leaving soon for the Valtellina via Menaggio. Though there were rumors he was going instead to Switzerland.

His convoy consisted of an armored car, a couple of Alfa Romeos, some Fiats, and assorted trucks and jeeps. About thirty or forty vehicles in all plus a contingent of twenty-two Waffen-SS troops and an SD detachment of plainclothes German security police. The SS had Schmeisser automatic rifles, two machine guns, and antitank weapons. Their commander, an Untersturmfuhrer-SS, rode in a Kubelwagen and his men in a battered old truck. The SD had two closed cars. In addition to these groups there were Il Duce's mistress, Claretta Petacci, her brother and his family, the dictator's son, Vittorio, and many of the Salo Republic Fascist bigwigs and their wives and children. Plus an assorted bunch of Black Shirts and Italian soldiers. To stop them we had only three carbines, a couple of Sten guns, five revolvers, a Thompson machine gun, six grenades, and some knives and .45s. And no gasoline.

So Salvatore and Giorgio skulked around town until they located several gallons of petrol and just in time too. At three-thirty with the cold rain falling harder

15

than ever the straggly line of vehicles cranked up to crawl through the twisting narrow streets. We watched from a doorway. Mussolini in a militia uniform passed by in the lead car followed by six other big fancy Alfa Romeos and some nondescript Fiats. Then came the Germans and a lumbering armored car with machine guns sticking out the sides and a 20mm in the swiveling turret. Finally, the Petaccis. I noticed a woman in the back seat dressed in mink as if she were ready for the opera. It was hard to believe that such a slow-moving, disorganized, weird mixture of kids, women, soldiers, and bureaucrats could be going anywhere.

Maybe if we had been able to round up a couple of hundred partisans in a hurry we might have stopped them. But there wasn't time to find anybody or develop any plan. So the captain decided that we would simply follow the motley crowd fleeing northward and wait for a chance to strike. He hadn't counted on the SS and SD and the armored car. Nor so many civilians. Their presence worried him for some reason. The others, too, looked concerned, especially when they saw how well armed the Germans were.

I thought about slipping away in the excitement and going to look for units of the First Armored Division supposed to be roaring up from the Po Valley through Brescia according to reports broadcast on the BBC. But every time I started to make my break I saw D'Alessandro eyeing me. Carlo and Bruno, too. One move to leave the truck and I would be a dead man. So I became resigned to follow the doomed caravan at least for a while. My only consolation was that it couldn't go very far, not at the speed it was traveling out of the city and the dozens of people joining and the frequent stops every mile or so. Eventually the whole line would have to halt for good either to surrender or regroup. And at that point there would be so much confusion it would be no problem to light out.

The whole lake area seemed to be in a flux anyway, Germans retreating in disorder for their lives, partisans coming down out of the hills and shooting anyone acting suspicious, the Allies driving up from the south with tanks faster and faster to liberate town after town. In no time the entire north would be swarming with Americans. Already I could hear our artillery booming in the distance.

Instead of calming the captain's fears the Allied advances made him more nervous. He didn't want anybody to reach Mussolini before he did, not the U.S. Army, not any partisan group, not even the CLNAI. And he was certain we would get the opportunity to take him if we were patient enough. Maybe not capture the big bastard alive, but certainly seize the Salò Republic's treasury and come away with if not all the gold at least most of it. What he planned to do with the loot he didn't say. Turn everything over to the Allies or the Communists, keep the stuff himself and divide it up among his friends? He just hinted that he was under orders but never said whose or what they were. Which made me curious about what he was up to and whom he was working for and what he was going to do with me when the time came. I kind of got the idea that everything had been pretty well planned from the beginning of the mission, from the major's murder and the capture of Il Duce and the gold to the race to beat everybody to the pot at the end of the rainbow.

It was interesting to see him change from a slogan-spouting party member into a rapacious renegade. No more talk of Wall Street leeches and imperialist warmongers and blood-thirsty dictators. Now it was kill the Fascist bums and grab their money and shoot anybody who stood in the way.

Town after town we inched through in low gear behind the ragged line of vehicles—Moltrasio, Laglio, Brienno, Argegno, Cadenabbia. The shapes of magnificent villas along the lake and on the hillsides loomed through the mist with their cypresses and parks and great walls. At Ospedaletto a Romanesque campanile with a Gothic belfry rose out of the darkness like some

17

abandoned lighthouse. And all around us guns were going off and tracers and flares and artillery shells were lighting up the sky.

Giorgio and Salvatore and I crouched under a tarpaulin in the back of the lorry while D'Alessandro, Carlo, and Bruno sat up front. The riding was rough with the rain coming down harder and harder and the truck hitting pothole after pothole and the partisans beside me bouncing around while smoking and jabbering. Whenever we stopped, they would jump out and take a leak and then scramble back under the shelter like kids, light a cigarette, and giggle. That's what struck me most about them from the beginning, how toughened they were to this life and yet how high-spirited and simple, too, as if they were on a camping trip.

Menaggio at six o'clock was mobbed. Trucks and cars and people everywhere along the main street causing traffic jams. Already vehicles were turning around and heading back down the lake toward Como. Men walking along the highway called out to us it was finito, tutto finito. Like a band of dispirited deserters. They laughed when we said we were going to join Il Duce and his march of Brigate Nere to the Valtellina.

We parked on a side street and stayed cooped up in the truck as dawn broke. Everything was beginning to seem kind of senseless and static now. Especially when we heard later in the morning that Mussolini and his party were leaving for Switzerland and staying only a few miles from the border at a small rundown hotel, Miravelle, in Grandola. But D'Alessandro was sure the old fart was bluffing. He would never leave his country no matter how desperate. He had too much pride, too much patriotism. Besides, the Swiss would never let him in anyway, and if he did cross the border they would intern him and he would be handed over to the Allies. And he could never endure the humiliation of a trial and imprisonment. Not after the glory and deification he had enjoyed. No, he would continue toward the Valtel-

18

lina or the new capital of the Salò Republic at Merano where the Germans had an embassy. Or it could be that he and Hitler had some secret hideout in Bavaria they were going to retreat to and hold out for peace on their terms.

As for the stories about ten thousand Fascists rallying around their leader, they turned out to be pure fabrication, the work of the Party secretary, Pavolini. His followers were shrinking fast, not growing. The people hovering around Il Duce now were those who had no place to go and who hoped for some miracle to restore their old power. Talk of a fabulous German secret weapon circulated too. But that sounded to the captain more like wishful thinking than anything else. No, wherever the old bastard looked now he would find a dead end and soon would have to stop, face the enemy, and accept his fate. That's when we'd hit him.

After spying around town, we spotted a little empty house on the northern outskirts across the road from the lake and settled down to wait for the next move from the convoy, which had to pass by us. I got out the radio and sent a message to Florence on the Guard Channel to indicate we were trailing Ben closely and should have him prisoner by the end of the week. The message I decoded in return read: "Silvio coming from Switzerland for Ben. Hold. Sending plane to Bassino airport, Milan. Surrender at Caserta Sunday."

D'Alessandro laughed at Corvo's words. We would take Il Duce in our own way or give him to the partisans and the hell with headquarters. This was our show now and nobody was telling us what to do. "Shit," he said, "let the CLNAI have his body if they want it so bad. They can't eat it, spend it, trade it. Only bury it. And even then they'll have to protect it from mutilation. He's good for only one thing now and that's his gold. Tomorrow, you guys, we make our move."

"Why tomorrow?" I asked.

"Because the longer he's on the road up here the more scavengers he's going to attract. Christ, everybody

19

on the lake must know by now where the hell he is and where he's going and how much money he's carrying. Partisans by the thousands will be converging on him. The Fifth Army will get the word and send a tank force. So our chances are getting fewer and fewer. It's tomorrow or never. Everybody agree?'' He looked at us in the little bare room with a weak light coming through the window. They all nodded.

"You mean or it'll all be for nothing," I said, looking directly at him through the dimness.

"You still worried about the major, Vic?" he turned on me.

"Yeah, it still bothers me. You didn't have to kill him that way."

"Forget it. It's just something that had to be done. He got sick at the wrong time. We couldn't let him fall in the Krauts' hands."

"You poisoned him."

"Nonsense. I've got witnesses to prove that happened."

"You guys killed him in cold blood. Just because he was trying to do what he was sent up here to do."

"Look, kid," he tensed and spat out at me, "you shut the hell up about the major now, you hear me, or I'm going to do something I don't want to do. He's dead and for a good reason that I can't go into here. We've got other things to worry about. Capeesh?" I lowered my head and gazed at the floor. Nobody in the room moved. I couldn't even hear any breathing.

It was a restless day, sporadic rain and rumors and nothing to do but wait for something to happen. The longer we sat in that airless, dusky house with few windows, cold and damp and depressed, waiting for the convoy to start moving again, the more I thought about escaping. Bruno and Carlo talked quietly to each other. Giorgio and Salvatore drank wine and smoked. D'Alessandro brooded. Occasionally a partisan darted in to tell us what Mussolini was doing up at Grandola and who was leaving and who was joining him and what his plans were for tomorrow. Nothing seemed certain, everything was in chaos. General Graziani had departed for Como in disgust. The Germans and Italians were constantly quarreling. Il Duce was moody, weary and resigned one moment and then stamping his feet and threatening the next and everybody acting scared as hell and nobody knowing what to do or where to go. Pavolini had brought back another armored car from Como along with twelve Black Shirts and the daughter of one of Mussolini's old mistresses. Already she and Claretta were hissing at one another. All I could think of was bedlam and bitchery.

Early that evening after supper I got discouraged myself and slipped out the back and went across the road to the lake. The mountains reared up on the other side like great shaggy beasts. Finding a rowboat with oars, I contemplated jumping in and escaping to the eastern shore that seemed pretty close. Once D'Alessandro captured Il Duce and grabbed the treasure and I sent the message that would be my finale. They couldn't let me hang around and talk to the Fifth Army.

I got in the boat and put the oars in the locks. The mist was turning to a heavy drizzle, reducing visibility. And just as I was about to undo the line and set out, the captain appeared out of the blackness to stand there on the dock like some grisly ghost, Sten gun in hand.

"You don't want to do that, Vic," he said softly, almost paternally. I gazed down at the water—cold, black, bottomless. "Not when everything is beginning to fall into place for us. We'll get him tomorrow, I promise you. And you'll get your share of the loot, don't worry."

"I don't want any part of the goddamn stuff."

"We'll see when the time comes. You might not have any choice in the matter."

"You mean you're going to make me an accomplice to this rotten scheme of yours?"

"Right, and you'll keep quiet about it too. Especially about the major's death. Nobody's going to find him.

21

And if they do they won't find much, not enough to identify him or discover how he died."

"I don't think that way. Sorry."

"You better for your own good."

"You mean you're planning a watery grave for me too?"

"Look, Vic, I'm going to level with you. None of all this is what it seems. Even I'm not. But I can't tell you a thing yet. Just trust me that I know what I'm doing and where I'm going."

"Who do you trust?"

"I can't tell you that. Only we're still in OSS and we're still on the Pontiac mission. Just the leadership has changed."

"You mean the direction, don't you? That's a lot of bull. The mission died with the major and you know it. You guys are out for the gold, not Mussolini. Don't kid me."

"I see there's no use trying to talk sense to you. Come on, let's get back to the house and wait for the convoy to start moving again." He waved the gun at me.

Though I couldn't see his face through the darkness, I imagined the little hard eyes, the cruel mouth. And I was convinced that if I hadn't gotten out of that boat, he would have shot me dead and walked away without giving it another thought.

We went back to the green-shuttered house overlooking the road. He talked about the Valtellina with its snow-capped peaks. What a beautiful sunny tropical paradise it was amid the Alps, full of magnificent flowers and grape vines, the source of the best wine in Italy. Too bad the Old Moose wouldn't spend his last years up there. But maybe we would get a glimpse of it before we sailed for home. How would I like that? I didn't answer him.

The two partisans were talking excitedly with Carlo and Bruno when we entered. Another group of Tedeschi had joined the convoy. A Luftwaffe communication unit with 160 men and some 30 trucks loaded with

22

weapons and telephone and telegraph equipment. There would now be well over a 100 vehicles in line with close to 200 armed men. More than enough to defeat any partisan force in the area. As far as I knew there was only one unit nearby, the Fifty-second Garibaldi Brigade in the hills above Dongo headed by a man named Pedro, and it was supposed to be scattered and weak. The Fifth Army from all reports hadn't entered Como yet. Maybe now Mussolini and his gang would get to their Shangri-la in the Alps, live off the fruit of the land, and settle for less than unconditional surrender.

The news disturbed the captain. For the first time I saw him lose his confident air, no doubt thinking he might have killed the major for nothing and maybe in the end be shot himself. And there would be no glory for trying to capture the dictator, no money, no successful conclusion to whatever enigmatic mission he was on. Certainly he couldn't attack a convoy over a mile long, not when it contained so many Krauts. And to bring in a couple of partisan brigades at this point, even if he could find them, would defeat his purpose. They would take credit for whatever victory followed and claim the spoils.

"Well, what are we going to do, go back to Como and wait for the Fifth Army?" I asked.

"No, we're keeping after them. Just the way I said. Don't worry. The Krauts aren't going to save Mussolini. They only want to save their own necks. Maybe we can make a deal with them. Get on your radio, Vic, and tell those goddamn 4 F's down in Florence we're about to take Il Duce."

"Take him?" I gaped at the muscular little guy standing in the middle of the room, candle light silhouetting his thick frame against the wall. "You're crazy. How? Where? With what? They've got machine guns, two armored cars, SS and Luftwaffe troops fully armed."

"Give me the map." Bruno took a roll from a knap-

23

sack and unwound it on the floor under the candle. The lines appeared like a giant spider web covering the country from Sicily to the Alps and stretching over the sea on both sides into Corsica on the left and Yugoslavia on the right.

"Okay, look here. There's Musso up ahead, maybe seventeen or eighteen kilometers. How about that place? Or better still look at Dongo about a mile further. It's got to be one of the two. Once he reaches Gravedona at the end of the lake he can head for the Valtellina and hole up and hold off an army for an eternity."

"But there's only six of us."

"Don't worry, the Krauts will desert him and take most of their weapons with them. The Eyeties will have to shift for themselves, and then they'll start fighting with each other. Remember, you guys, this is the end of the war. It's every man for himself. The Krauts know they're finished. They just want to get home. They're not going to stand around and sacrifice themselves for some beaten old son-of-a-bitch they never got along with anyway. They'd probably like to see him fall into our hands just to get rid of him. What do you say, Salvatore, Giorgio?" The two partisans grinned without quite understanding him, I was certain. Bruno and Carlo nodded and appeared ready to go. The only thing that worried them was the armored cars. If Il Duce rode in one of them, it might be hard to stop him. They didn't have any antitank guns or mines. Maybe grenades would do it. The steel plate didn't look too thick.

As I went to sleep in my bag that night, I kept thinking how crazy everything was becoming. Here I was the son of a high school chemistry teacher from Albany, New York, on the trail of the infamous dictator I used to see in the Fox Movie-tone News every Saturday afternoon at the Madison just before Rin Tin Tin. The arm-waving maniac on the screen seemed then as remote as anybody could be, up there on that little balcony

24

lording it over the thousands cheering below. And now here he was just a couple of miles away fleeing for his life with me after him. No crowds or speeches or army. Just a rag-tag group of desperate hangers-on trying to beat it north to some safe haven with every lira they could lay their hands on. And he no leader anymore. Just a doomed old man.

"You awake, Vic," the captain leaned over me. "Let's go and talk somewhere. I got an idea." I struggled out of the sack and followed him through the door and down steps into a chilly, damp cellar. He lit a candle and put it on a box. I had the queerest feeling this might be it. He lines me up against the wall and pop goes the weasel.

"Listen, I just thought of something. How about you joining the convoy when it starts again this morning?"

"Me? How? Why? My Italian's not that good. All right for the States and talking to partisans in pigdin English. But not here. My accent's wrong for the region. I'd have to put on civilian clothes. No more protection from the Geneva code."

"You wouldn't have to say anything. Just get in one of the lorries for a ride. You can change clothes with Salvatore. He's your size. Besides, nobody's going to notice you. There'll be too many people."

"Suppose I'm taken by the partisans?"

"We'll be right behind to get you out of anything like that."

"I don't know." I looked away. "You thinking of getting rid of me this way? The partisans or the Krauts shoot me by mistake and no blood on your hands."

"Look, Vic, you've got me all wrong. Maybe I have been a little sharp with you, acted a little tough. I don't blame you for thinking about me the way you do because of what I did to the major. But I had my reasons for taking care of him. Believe me. Now I need you in that convoy if we're ever going to lay our hands on the big prick and his gold when the partisans attack. And they're going to. I just got word. Tomorrow

25

morning north of here. I'm not certain where yet."

"What about the others? They speak the language better than I do. They're more experienced in this sort of thing. You can trust them."

"They don't have it upstairs. I need someone with brains, someone who can think for himself. They can take orders, but they can't operate on their own."

"Aren't you afraid I might try to escape?"

"Where would you go? Across the lake? To Switzerland? And we'll be keeping tabs on you."

"But what's the point of my riding in a truck? What can I do? I don't get it frankly."

"Spy on them. Find out which car the big Moose is in, what truck has the gold, so when we stop them we can go right in there and take what we want before anybody knows what's going on. Once the shooting starts and the rout is on everybody and his brother is going to get into the act."

"I don't know."

"You've got to, Vic. Jesus, don't forget there's supposed to be nearly half a billion in the convoy. It's the chance of a lifetime for all of us, you, me, OSS, the Allies, Italy. Enough for everybody. You Capeesh? And every mother-fucking son-of-a-bitch is going to be after it."

"Is that what the Pontiac mission is all about?"

"One of the things. So get going."

"Do I have a choice?"

"Not really. Either you join the convoy the way I said or we'll dump you in the lake." His jaw was set. He stared through me with those hard black eyes.

It sounded bizarre. But then so did everything that had happened so far, from his killing the major to our pursuing these refugees from a lost war. What could be crazier anyway than helping a gang of crooks rob a whole government as part of a secret mission led by a Communist? And yet I knew that if I kept playing along with him the greater would be my chances of living to tell the fantastic story one day. And maybe, just maybe, he was giving me the straight truth and it all did have something to do with a genuine official mission. I could be misinterpreting his motives, misreading his actions. And he could be misleading me just to throw off the others. An odd guy all right, one moment cajoling me, the next threatening. Intelligent yet brutal as hell. When he looked at you it was like facing a firing squad.

"Okay, when do I start?"

"We've got a driver in the convoy right now who says he'll help us. Salvatore's gone to see him. He'll explain you want a ride to Dongo, that's all. You won't have to say a word. Just look like a native."

"And a Fascist?"

He laughed and patted me on the back. "That should be easy. You look like the perfect Black Shirt with that dark skin and black hair and big chin."

"I'm beginning to feel like one all right."

"What's that supposed to mean?" he snapped at me.

"Nothing. Just talking to myself."

"Keep your thoughts to yourself. And don't worry. We'll keep the radio for you. Everything's going to work out fine. By this time tomorrow we'll be telling the world we captured Il Duce and ended Fascism forever. We'll be making history."

I followed him back upstairs and went over to the window to look out at the narrow road and the lake across the way, too keyed up to go back to sleep. It was a bleak town all right and even a bleaker spring morning, freezing and wet and murky. Somehow it didn't feel like the end of the war. No exhilaration, no relief. And as for going back home and entering law school and living a normal life again, that all seemed farther off than ever.

"What do you see?" D'Alessandro came over and put an arm around me.

"Nothing. Just realizing what a hell of a world this is."

"You just finding that out, Vic. God help you! Just don't think about it too much."

27

"I'll try not to." He left me standing there alone listening to the wind and the distant guns. A truck moved past the house shaking the foundation, the headlights picking their way through the fog. Then silence, darkness, emptiness, and thoughts of home.

Chapter 3

The captain woke me at four. Mussolini had spent the night at the schoolhouse barracks down the road after leaving Hotel Miravelle in Grandola yesterday afternoon. Apparently he couldn't get into Switzerland and had returned to Menaggio to continue the desperate journey to the Valtellina. The convoy, or what was left of it after rumored desertions, was forming. Already motors were roaring and people were stirring and you could hear the bustling and shouting and stamping of feet.

Outside it was still rainy and foggy. The room felt cold as ever. Salvatore came in, and we exchanged clothes silently by candlelight. His brown trousers and leather jacket fitted perfectly. I slipped my .45, several packs of cigarettes, and a wad of lire into the pockets. The civvies seemed strange. I hadn't worn any in over two years. And the shirt and pants were thin. I was freezing my ass off even with the jacket and a hat. I began to regret that I had ever agreed to the plan and was becoming more and more suspicious that this was the way the captain planned to get rid of me. Salvatore stood there in my uniform grinning away and pointing to the dog tags around my neck. But I wasn't giving up those. Christ, I had to keep some kind of identity in this mess.

We went out back where the others were waiting. Carlo and Bruno stood against the wall, carbines slung over their shoulders. Giorgio carried a Thompson machine gun. He wore a bandoleer for the first time and reminded me of pictures I had seen of Pancho Villa in Mexico.

"Now don't forget, Vic," the captain said, "if the partisans take you, show them your dog tags and tell them we're right behind the convoy and can identify you. And keep your eye out for all the valuables that are supposed to be in those trucks. It's a rolling Fort Knox. Bruno and Carlo and I are going ahead to Dongo to look for the leader of the Fifty-second Garibaldi Brigade, some guy called Pedro. He's supposed to be in charge of setting the trap for old Ben and his buddies. Giorgio and Salvatore are going to follow the convoy in the truck."

"Okay," I said. "Let's go. I'm ready as I'll ever be I guess."

"One thing more. Come over here." He took me aside out of the hearing of the others. "Do a good job for us, Vic. The others wanted to shoot you back at the villa, throw your body in the lake with the major's. I saved your hide. I said you deserved a chance to help us. So you do it and show them. Me too. You've got the stuff. I know you'll do a good job for us." He patted me on the back.

I grunted in the affirmative. He called Salvatore over, and we left through a dark, black alley for the center of town.

It was a longer and more crowded convoy than I expected. At the head loomed one of the two old armored cars with large wheels and steel plates, iron-shuttered windows, and a cluster of machine guns. It reminded me of a mammoth beetle squatting there. Next came a green Alfa Romeo and Mussolini standing beside the vehicle in the glare of the headlights from the trucks. It was my first full glimpse of him in the flesh, although I suppose I had been carrying around his picture in my head ever since I could remember. One of those images from movies and newspapers that become part of you—the chin thrust out, the wide stance, the black boots, the riding crop, the hand held high over cheering thousands below. Now he wore a gray tunic, black shirt, breeches with twin red and black stripes down the side, jackboots, a gray forage cap. He held a small machine gun. A heavier and shorter and older man than I had imagined, flabby, deep-lined face, cropped head, slack mouth.

People kept coming up to him and talking feverishly, and he greeted each one in a resigned, weary, impassive way. Listening to their chatter like a man condemned to carry out a role that he had become tired of and that no one really believed in anymore either despite the excitement. And for a second I felt sorry for him. He was definitely over-the-hill, used up, finished, ready to be tossed out on the garbage heap of history and buried in some dump. It would be impossible for him to continue much longer given his present state and situation. Either he'd end up an Allied prisoner mocked by his own bravado or a corpse torn to pieces by the enemy.

A small, dark-haired woman in a fur coat approached, the same one I had seen back in Como. He hugged her in a limp way. She babbled on with gestures while he stood vaguely attentive. Then she left and civilians and officers clustered around once more.

Behind his Alfa Romeo came the SS jeep and a lorry of German soldiers and then more trucks, the other armored vehicle, and more cars and trucks. After this group waited still another line of German vehicles that Salvatore said belonged to a Luftwaffe communications unit. The men wore blue uniforms with brown collar tabs. Certainly a hodge-podge if there ever was one, stretching from one end of the town to the other. It reminded me of a combination carnival and National Guard outfit on the way to summer camp complete with women and children. Frantic shouting, motorcycles gunning their engines, trucks starting, people running up and down the line waving lanterns, Italian and German voices clashing. An incredible scene of confusion and cacophony. The racket became almost deafening. And watching the whole mad business were spectators dressed in heavy coats huddled on the side peering through the drizzle and mist—silent, curious, bewildered.

Like something out of Dante's *Inferno*, I thought, the more I looked at the convoy. Almost surrealistic. A terrific frenzy about the milling around and the noise and the lights, yet everything strangely static. As if everyone knew they were going nowhere despite the feverish preparations and the desperate haste to be off.

Salvatore led me through the throng of civilians and Italian and German soldiers to a truck down the line. He got in the cab after me and introduced the driver dressed in a leather jacket and cap and hunched over the wheel —slight frame, oval face, dark hair, small hands. I said, "Buon giorno," and gazed into the eyes shaded by the cap and faintly lit by the headlights of the trucks behind us warming up their engines.

"My God, signorina!" I burst out.

"Si, si," she smiled, scarcely opening her mouth, her voice almost inaudible.

"Bruna," Salvatore said. He explained that her brother, Enrico, was a partisan in Dongo. "She help you, Sergeant. Buono, molto buono."

"Parla Inglese?"

"Ah, si, si," she said, "un po.'"

Salvatore patted me on the shoulder and slipped out of the cab and melted away in the mob.

"Anybody know you're here?"

"Do not worry, Signor, they no look in lorry. Not long to Dongo. Partigiani come. They help us. Okay?"

"You mean it's all planned? They're going to attack the convoy? Ambush it?"

"Non capisco."

"Capture Mussolini."

"Ah, si, not capture. Shoot. You help, no? Americano. You not like Il Duce. You shoot too."

"The Allies want him alive, not dead. No execution. And they want the gold."

32

"No gold. We have gold."

"Where is it?" She glanced over her shoulder, and I looked around and saw through the small window cases piled up on top of each other in the open area. "You mean you're driving the whole treasury from Salò? Everything is here?"

"Ah, si, Signor. Buono, no? We guard it." She smiled at me with that tight little mouth. Her eyes were small but awfully bright and friendly.

"Where are they stopping the convoy?"

"Dongo."

'How? They'll have to have an army. There must be over two hundred Tedeschi here, and they're well armed."

"You see. It is a surprise. Morte ai Fascisti. Morte al Duce. No more Grigate Nere, squadristi, gerarchi. Libertà ai popoli."

"You Communista?"

"I am Bruna, Signor. No Communista, no socialista, Bruna, Bruna." She looked grimly ahead, her fingers tight around the wheel.

The vehicles began to move. She switched on the engine, shifted into gear, and we inched forward with a couple of jerks. It was about a quarter to six and still foggy and rainy. A few people continued to stand and watch us pass as if we were part of a parade. Shutters along the route opened partially on each side of the road emitting light and then closing quickly. By the time we reached the outskirts, there was no one on the sidelines, only blank stone buildings.

We moved slowly at a jogging pace, rolling through town after town—Rezzonico, Cremia, Calozzo, Lovezzano. Always the same cluster of little stone structures bunched up against the hills and beside the lake—the town hall, the church, the urinal, the statue or war memorial or fountain in the square, the low wall and the fishing jetty. Snaking through narrow streets and skirting water, hugging sheer rock faces and groping in and out of tunnels and under and over bridges. The sky

33

gradually lightened. The noise of the vehicles created one continuous roar. It was as if the war were receding farther and farther and we were traveling through a country desolate, melancholy, timeless.

At first Bruna didn't say a word, concentrating on the driving, but as darkness thinned out and I could see her more clearly, she opened up. She reminded me of those squat Yugoslav partisan girls that I had seen in Bari last August promenading up and down along the harbor in British battle dress with hand grenades dangling from their belts. Except she looked more feminine with her large breasts and moist lips and dark eyebrows.

"You from Dongo?"

"Si."

"Partisan?"

"Si. My father, my mother dead. Tedeschi, Fascisti bad, no good, Signor. I hate them. You too, no?" She looked straight ahead as she talked, never relaxing her body or her hands on the wheel. Although not more than eighteen or nineteen there was a fierce sort of determination in that round youthful face, I thought, and a sort of suppressed sexiness too. And I recalled Mussolini's mistress whom I had seen back in Menaggio. The two were about the same size. But no fur coat on Bruna, only a ragged jacket, trousers, heavy men's shoes, hair pulled back under the cap, no makeup. She probably had been fighting Germans and Fascists and living with partisans in the hills around here for a couple of years. And after the war she would continue to work with the Reds, maybe even become a leader of one of their cells and ignore the whole idea of a family, live the revolutionist's dream and one day die on some lonely street unmartyred, unknown.

The convoy stopped at Acquaseria. Clusters of the curious gathered along the side of the road, mostly old men and women in shabby coats and shawls and kerchiefs. A few dogs and children too. Mussolini got out of his big car and stood beside it, feet spread apart, hands on hips, chin pushed out, the old familiar pose.

34

He spoke a few words. It was a showy performance, well rehearsed and sort of mechanical. The people cheered. And the old guy did look impressive in his gray-green uniform and red and black striped knickers and black boots, as if nothing had changed over the years. Only a little dustier and more wrinkled. A contrast to the dispirited convoy stalled along the street like vehicles snarled in traffic. Then he turned and walked forward to the lead armored car. Another cheer broke out. He gave the Fascist salute to the crowd before disappearing behind the steel plates.

"When do we reach Dongo?" I asked Bruna.

"Subito, subito. We go to Musso and then Dongo. There we see partigiani."

"There's going to be a battle?"

"You see. I not know. We wait."

"What'll we do if they start shooting at us?"

"Enrico help us. He is in Dongo."

"And he'll help us with the cases in the back?"

"After they kill Mussolini."

"What about Americani?"

"They want gold?"

"That's what they're doing up here. That's why I'm riding with you, to find out where it is, protect it, lead them to it when the time comes. They couldn't care less about Il Duce."

"No, no, Italiani get gold, not Americani."

"They plan to give it to the Allies. Maybe even keep some for themselves."

"No, no, Italiani get gold. Capisce?"

I did and I didn't. But I said no more, thinking how the captain would react when he found out that he was working with a patriotic partisan rather than a party member.

The line started up again, hesitantly, stalling for a moment, then grinding and thundering forward. The drizzle continued. The lake loomed gray among the steep sodden hills. And it was freezing inside the cab. I jammed my hands into my pockets, but still couldn't keep warm. Bruna never took her eyes off the truck in front, hunched over the wheel as if part of it. Nothing seemed to distract her. She sat so still, so stiff, so determined with that fixed mouth and those eyes focused on the rear lights of the lorry ahead.

We passed through Musso and started to climb the hill outside of town on the way to Dongo. On the right a sharp drop to the water, on the left a steep rockside. At the top of the rise the road went around a sweeping curve where a huge boulder jutted out.

As the creaky old armored car approached the rock, it halted. Thirty yards ahead lay a pile of stones and logs. Then it started to move forward and rammed into the wall on the right as machine guns rattled away and flattened the tires. The whole line shuddered to a standstill. Women and children screamed and scattered. Soldiers and civilians popped out of their vehicles and scurried down the hill to Musso. All of a sudden I could envisage cars and trucks exploding and flames leaping up and the holocaust spreading the length of the convoy.

"This it?" I said.

"Si, Vall'Orba. We wait." She ducked down behind the wheel. I dropped to the floor.

"Your brother Enrico come now?"

"Subito, subito."

We crouched for a couple of minutes below the dashboard listening to the gunfire, bullets zinging overhead, pinging against the trucks and cars, shattering glass. Most of the shooting seemed to be coming from the partisans on the hill, only a few shots fired from the lorries and armored cars. When everything stopped, I got out and looked around. The lead armored car squatted helpless before the blockade, its guns silent except for a few sporadic rounds. Behind us the line stretched down into the streets of Musso like some enormous snake that had grown ominously still.

Bruna got out and stood beside me. Partisans with a white flag came forward and began talking to the

Germans. Yet no one emerged from the armored car where Mussolini remained secluded with most of the Fascists.

"What do we do now?" I turned to her.

"Wait. You see. Tedeschi will give up. They know it is finito. They go home. They do not die in Italia. They do not fight to defend Il Duce. Capisce, Signor?"

"Does anyone know you're carrying the whole Fascist tesor?"

"No, only Fascisti. And they do not show themselves. They use gold to buy their lives from partigiani. Possible Mussolini's life too, no? But it is no good. They have nothing now. They die and we have gold. Buono, Signor."

"What about the Italian government? They want the gold, don't they?"

"No, we give it only to partigiani."

"So you won't give it to the Allies either when they come?"

"No."

"That could be considered stealing. You could have the American army after you."

"You stop us, Signor?"

"I might if I have to."

"And Il Duce, you stop us from shooting him?"

"He's supposed to be a prisoner of the Allies. They want to try him for war crimes." She laughed, a hard, deep-throated laugh.

Just then a German officer and a group of partisans left the convoy for Dongo, driving around the dismantled barrier and down the hill. Mussolini climbed out of the armored car and started talking with both German and Italian officers. They were arguing with him, and he was shouting, waving his arms, sticking out that big chin. Abruptly, he broke off the conversation and climbed back into the vehicle. A couple of minutes passed and a small figure in blue overalls and wearing a helmet over dark curly hair entered the car. Then everything became calm for an hour or so until finally he emerged again, this time wearing a Luftwaffe coat and a Kraut helmet. He paused for a moment to look around and walked straight back to the fourth lorry and climbed in among the German soldiers.

"You see?" Bruna grinned at me in that fiercely gritty way of hers.

"He could get away with it."

"No, no, we see him. He not escape. It is finito Il Duce and Fascisti. They die today."

For another hour we stood by the side of the road expecting something to happen. Either the convoy to start moving ahead down the hill or a band of partisans to descend and take everybody prisoner. Gunfire broke out in the direction of the town, a short burst. Then a kind of unreal stillness settled over the line of vehicles. The Germans stood around smoking and talking and trading cigarettes for wine with a woman from Musso pushing casks in a wheelbarrow up the hill. More people drifted away from the convoy, although no one came out of the armored car. A perfect place for an ambush all right with a steep hill on one side and a long drop to the lake on the other and no room to turn around.

"Will they shoot him?"

"Il Duce e Fascisti, tutti, tutti. They die. You not know, Signor, what terrible things they do to people, my family, friends. All dead now. Only Enrico and I left. Bad, very bad."

"What about me? What will the partisans do with me?"

"They will not hurt you. You are Americano. They let you go."

"But if they steal the gold and I report it to the Allies?"

"They shoot you." She looked directly at me.

"You mean by a firing squad?"

"Si, the way Tedeschi do. They line all people against the wall and shoot them down, boom, boom, boom, even bambini. I see, I know. Tedeschi come to town, take men, women, shoot them in piazza, in church."

We got back in the truck, and she told me about her experiences fighting with the partisans, sickening, frightening experiences that, although familiar enough, became in her broken English somehow startling and gripping and heartrending. Villages wiped out, entire areas left lifeless, children homeless without parents. For the first time the devastation of war came home to me. Slowly, inevitably tears glistened in her eyes. She stopped speaking to control herself. I leaned over and kissed her on the cheek. She stared at me and said softly, "Grazie, Signor, grazie," as if I had given her lire or a piece of bread. It was one of those quiet moments in the midst of a maelstrom you never forget when everything becomes absolutely still inside and out just one second before all hell breaks loose.

About three o'clock the German jeeps and lorries began to move down the steep hill into Dongo past the barricade. We remained stationary. Only the crippled armored car came alive trying to turn around, firing wildly and resembling an insect writhing in the throes of dying. A grenade exploded beside it, and the car, after moving ahead a few feet, went crashing again into the wall along the lakeside. Fascists jumped out and were immediately seized. Only one of them, whom Bruna identified as Pavolini, attempted to escape by leaping into the water. But he too was caught and marched with the others down into the town.

"We get them now," Bruna turned to me after the frenzied action died down. "Even Il Duce. We get them, tutti, tutti."

"What will they do with me?"

"You not worry. Enrico come."

"You going to hand over all the cases back there?"

"Si, to partigiani I know, Enrico know. We hide them in church."

"What if they're Communisti?"

She didn't answer. A partisan hopped on our running board and told her to drive behind the Tedeschi to the piazza. She started the motor, and we rolled carefully around Vall'Orba and crept down the hill to the small square with the bay and the jetty on one side and the town hall on the other. Hundreds of people stood scrutinizing us, and for a moment I felt as if I were one of the condemned. So many strange, hostile faces pressing toward the truck, so many fists shaking and rifles waving and curses exploding against us. I kept glancing at Bruna and wondering when she was going to declare herself and reveal who we were. She knew these people. She could talk to them, explain my situation. But she stayed fixed in her seat behind the wheel, a little half-smile playing over her face. And I wondered if this was why I had been put here by the captain, not to find or spot the gold but to be done away with.

"What now?" I whispered as we parked in the midst of a mob.

"We wait, Signor. We wait."

"For what? For these maniacs to attack us? They don't act too friendly."

"Till they find Il Duce in the lorry." And her mouth parted in a broad toothy smile.

Chapter 4

The instant Mussolini stumbled out of the Luftwaffe truck, helmet off, there was a gasp and then wild, angry shouting. He acted weighted down under the German overcoat that he unbuttoned to show a dusty, baggy Fascist uniform. Resignation was written all over his face. Quickly, the partisans rushed him through the crowd and under the Norman arch of the town hall. People pressed toward the building, yelling, jeering, even firing a few shots. I thought surely they were going to storm the place and string him up.

The end of an era all right. But the whole thing was happening so fast it felt more like the end of a game with the coaches and players running off the field to prevent being trampled by the people surging around them.

A group of partisans gathered beside our truck to ask for my identity. I handed over my dog tags, proclaiming myself Americano. They acted skeptical and made me get out and follow two guards. I protested and pleaded with Bruna to intervene and explain the situation. She shrugged her shoulders and sat silent in the cab as they led me off to the town hall behind a group of Fascists. Inside, we passed a large room on the ground floor where Mussolini was talking calmly, quietly to some armed men around a table, answering their questions about the war and his Italian policies. He looked pale and haggard in his gray militia uniform. My cell was a small dark room that faced the square and the lake.

After I had been locked up for a couple of hours, a tall mustached partisan came to see me. Why was I being held? I wasn't a Fascist or a sympathizer. I had nothing to do with Mussolini. An OSS radio operator for the Pontiac Mission at Lake Orta. At first he pretended not to understand. Then he admitted that they were holding me because someone told them I wanted to have Il Duce handed over to the Allies on Sunday along with all his ministers and the whole treasury.

"So you're going to shoot him?"

"No, no," he said excitedly, "we have trial. We let him speak. We give him justice."

"And his gold?"

"It belong to people."

"You mean to the Communist Party," I said, noticing the red armband and the red neckerchief. "Part of your plan to set up a Red state here."

"You do not like Communista, Signor? We try you, too, with Il Duce and gerarchi."

"How long are you planning to hold me?"

"Until everything finito."

"You better get in touch with the Fifth Army then. You do anything to me and they'll be up here with tanks and planes and blow this place off the map." He laughed and left.

The afternoon dragged on into Friday evening. The crowds outside in the square grew uglier and more threatening. And I could imagine a frenzied few by nightfall breaking in and killing every damn one of us without pausing to ask for identification. Like a lynch mob in a Western.

After dark, Mussolini, under constant harrassment, was transferred to a hamlet up in the hills above Dongo. The news traveled fast through the huge building, and prisoners on the ground floor with me began grumbling and shouting. The tumult outside increased too. Any moment I expected a mob to break in and drag me into the square for a public execution.

A guard came to my room to fetch me, and we

hurried out the back door to a waiting Fiat.

"Where the hell are you taking me? To be shot?"

"Germasino in mountains. You be safe. Il Duce there. Buono."

It was about eight o'clock when we reached the town via a steep winding road. The air terribly cold. Rainy and misty. I felt numb. And no Bruna. Now it was becoming increasingly obvious that she and Salvatore and the captain had set me up so I wouldn't live to tell the truth about the major's death or the plot to seize the Fascist treasury.

Luckily, though, the guard on my room in the police barracks was young and friendly and had relatives in the States and knew a few words of English. Besides, he hadn't had a cigarette in weeks. I bribed him with a couple and told him I needed a car right away. Could he help? He went off and came back and in no time I was a free man with transportation. But I couldn't take off from the jail. A couple of Fiats pulled up the moment I settled behind the wheel. Three men rushed out talking in excited, hushed tones about Mussolini. Suddenly the weary old man stumbled from the building, his head wrapped in a white bandage, a blanket over his shoulder, and got into one of the cars and took off down the road toward the lake. I followed. They stopped on a bridge where another Fiat waited, headlights blazing, and a woman in a fur coat and driver's cap stepped out and walked up to the dictator in his gray-green militia uniform. They talked for a minute and then retreated to their vehicles. And the little convoy took off down the Como highway.

It was tough going with the rain and the gunfire and the partisan checkpoints that I had to bribe my way through with cigarettes and lire. Everything unfamiliar in the darkness, the road blurry, landmarks dim and strange. At first I was just following them to find my way south to the Fifth Army. But when they turned off into the hills a few miles north of Como, I turned off with them and drove along a treacherous rutty road past

Azzano and then halted just short of Mezzegra where the pavement became a path. Mussolini, looking like a wounded soldier with his bandaged head, got out first. The woman in the mink and high heels accompanied him. They walked unsteadily up steep steps between low walls, the rain driving down and flooding their route. They looked beaten and wet like dogs just out of the water. Thunder and lightning everywhere. Then through a field and up to a small whitewashed farm house set against the hill and lit up by a quick jagged flash. A guard made a shrill sound, and a woman with an oil lamp appeared in the doorway. The whole party advanced and went in.

For a long time I waited under a tree with the thunder rattling and the rain beating down until all the partisans but two had driven away. I walked up to the door and rapped. A guard with a rifle opened it. I told him that I was an American sent here by General Clark and President Roosevelt to see Il Duce. If he didn't let me in, I would call the American Fifth Army at Como to come and surround the place with tanks and kill everybody who refused to surrender.

The partisan looked frightened and led me into a big rough room with a stone floor, barren except for a couple of straw-seated chairs, a table, a bench, and a barrel. A man and his wife and two boys and another guard stood in the middle gaping at me. No sign of Mussolini and his mistress. I pointed upstairs. The guard who let me in nodded, and taking an oil lamp from the table, I mounted the steps and slowly opened the door. It was a small room with whitewashed walls, a red brick floor, and a single window. The furniture consisted of a walnut bed, a washstand with an enamel bowl and pitcher and a steel mirror, and two cane chairs. On the wall over the headboard hung the painting of a Madonna and the picture of a World War I Alpine soldier. Mussolini and Claretta were in bed, only his shaven head showing above the covers. He told me to get out, leave them alone. What did I want anyway?

I explained in my broken Italian that I wasn't a partisan but an Americano who had come to take him and his friend to the American lines. Unless they accompanied me now they would be shot tomorrow. I had heard talk in Dongo of a firing squad.

The jowly gray old man sat up and gaped at me, shrunken-looking, thin naked shoulders, wrinkled neck. The woman popped up beside him in her underclothes, the dark curly hair and bulging breasts, gray-green eyes and short teeth. She tried to smile but was too scared and vanished under the covers. I started to leave. Suddenly he called me back and asked if I was alone. When I told him I was, he wanted to know how I could get past the guards. I held out a pack of cigarettes. He frowned.

"Okay, capisce?" I said. He continued to stare at me. Somehow the sad little guy under the Madonna and the Alpine soldier didn't seem to be the same one I had seen pictures of in the newspapers and the Fox Movietone News. Too feeble, too sallow-faced. I urged him to get dressed and hurry. He didn't move.

Footsteps sounded on the stairs—hard, quick steps. I turned just as a burly partisan burst through the doorway, a Sten gun in hand, and demanded I surrender. He grabbed the oil lamp and pushed me toward the stairwell. Thunder cracked overhead, rain pelted on the roof. The peasants and the guards were waiting at the bottom of the stairs. After slamming the bedroom door on the prisoners, the partisan plunged down after me.

"What are you going to do?" I confronted him. "Shoot me? If you are, you better hurry. The Fifth Army will be here pretty soon. I'm with OSS working with the Second Garibaldi Division over in the Lake Orta region. Capisce?"

He ordered me to sit down on the bench, still not saying anything. Nobody did. It was crazy. All of them around me showing their weapons and not uttering a word. Then the red-faced woman brought me some milk and cheese and hard biscuits and I started eating by myself, the six of them watching as if I were a creature from another world.

Evidently they didn't know what to do, whether to execute me on the spot, wait for orders, or let me go. Retreating to the other room, they conferred in whispers and came back. It was a standoff. While Il Duce and his mistress slept maybe the last sleep of their lives and not in the Palazzo Venezia but in a peasant hovel up in the mountains, I sat on a crude bench breaking bread with myself in front of a mystified audience.

The morning dragged on. Little by little darkness faded into day, and soon it was lunchtime and then afternoon. And now I found myself eating polenta with milk and feeling hungrier and hungrier the more I ate. Only one guard on me, the couple and their sons out in the fields, and the rough partisan with the Sten off to God knows where. The rain had ceased, and there were patches of blue sky. A brisk wind blew. I tried to think what day it must be and couldn't for the longest time. Then it hit me—Saturday, April 28, 1945. Christ, I had been on the road since Wednesday and on this earth twenty-three years and two months. I could be the son of the old guy up there.

It was funny they didn't tie me up or lock me in a closet or take away my clothes. Instead they let me sit there in the middle of the biggest room in the house brooding and eating, standing and stretching, gazing out the window at the peasants working in the field, pacing up and down in front of the stairs. Occasionally the guard took me in back to the outhouse and I stayed as long as I could and enjoyed the privacy and the sensation of parking my can on the same seat that Il Duce and his woman occupied. But the hours dragged, and I began to wonder if my fate now wasn't somehow tied to theirs.

Around mid-afternoon the guards began babbling. I looked up the stairs expecting Big Ben and his woman to descend for the last time. They didn't show. Only silence. What stirred the two partisans was a rumor that

46

some CLNAI men from Milano were coming to bring Mussolini back to the city for a people's trial. And they would be here any minute.

I checked the doors and windows, studied the two kids in their late teens or early twenties—tall, fresh-looking, genial, grinning—wondering how to get to them. I offered bribes, first cigarettes, then lire, finally a promise to take them to America after the war. Nothing worked. Neither did threats about the Fifth Army coming disturb them anymore. Since the Americani hadn't arrived after all this time, why should they show up now? Actually they seemed determined to make no move until the men from Milano appeared. And there was no use arguing with them.

Mussolini and Claretta never left their room except to go to the outhouse. Once the stocky peasant woman brought them up some food, and I could hear them walking around and mumbling. Every time I tried to go and see how they were doing the guards stopped me. So I gave up and stretched out on the bench and tried to sleep, aware of every noise.

About four o'clock a tall, dark nervous man in a brown raincoat, blue beret, and red neckerchief stormed into the house followed by two others in blue berets carrying machine pistols, one wearing a white raincoat and glasses and looking more studious than violent. They demanded Il Duce. I stood up to block them, and the leader with the clipped mustache and long sallow face, Colonel Valerio, wanted to know who I was. I told him, showing off my dog tags and insisting I was a friend of Pedro, head of the Fifty-second Garibaldi Brigade in Dongo. He wasn't impressed, brandishing his weapon, spitting out Italian with incredible speed. Two of his men pushed me aside.

"You shoot him and the whole Fifth Army will be on your necks," I shouted. They shoved me hard against the wall. I slipped and fell.

The leader bounded up the stairs to Mussolini's room and then rushed down with his two prisoners, both looking bewildered. The old man had on his gray-green uniform with the black shirt, jackboots, and forage cap. The woman wore her mink, a driver's cap, and high heels. I noticed she carried no pocketbook. The whole thing reminded me of a silent movie—a whitewashed hovel in the mountains, a great leader and his amante coming down from their nest where after fifteen years they had finally spent their last night together in the same bed. He appeared even feebler than he had earlier, the deeply lined, sunken face with the gray stubble, the hollow eyes. A paunchy, stooped figure. She, although her face was tear-swollen and weary, still maintained some of her famous allure—the dark hair and skin, the wide grayish-green eyes, the sensuous breasts accentuated by the white ruffled blouse. She propped up her lover as he stumbled across the room toward the door. And behind them the impatient man from Milan with the machine pistol urging the pair to hurry if they wanted to escape to Switzerland. There wasn't much time. He was grim.

"He's going to kill you, Il Duce," I said as he limped past. "No liberazione. Morte, morte. It's a goddamn trick." The guy in the raincoat screamed at me to get away and be quiet, thrusting a pistol in my face and letting loose a flood of obscenities which he delivered with machine-gun rapidity. I backed off. The woman opened her mouth as if to protest, showing those short teeth and no gums, fear in her bloodshot eyes. And I scrutinized the doll-like face and the makeup and the rings and the locket, smelled the lilac-scented perfume, heard one of the Milan partisans speak to a guard about her delaying them upstairs because she insisted on putting on her underpants. No movie star. Not even a great beauty. But there was a defiance in her feminity that touched me. She wasn't running away or pleading for her life. She was holding up her lover to the end, guiding him, encouraging him. He acted as if he were in a stupor.

"Americano, grazie, grazie," she paused beside me

48

and said in a low, throaty voice.

Before I could respond, the leader beckoned me to join the two prisoners.

"No, no," I shouted. "Americano. OSS. No Fascista."

He pointed his gun at me and went into another rhetorical rage, eyes blazing, hands going, his voice almost at the point of shrieking. I thought he was going to fire, and I set myself for the first bullet.

"Vieni, vieni," he hollered. The five men in the room moved toward me. I froze and then slowly fell behind Il Duce and Claretta Petacci, both silent now and shuffling along, she still supporting him and whispering something in Italian that seemed like, "I told you I would follow you to the end."

We walked down the hill through a meadow to a lane, under an archway, and between gray houses to a cobblestoned square. Three stout women were washing clothes in a trough and an old man was carrying a bundle of hay on his shoulders. Along the road trooped a group of women and children. Everything so Italian, so primitive, so normal.

A driver waited beside a black Fiat with a red flag in front. I got in back with the two prisoners. Colonel Valerio hopped on the right running board facing us with his pistol pointed inside the car. The man in the white raincoat walked ahead with a Dongo partisan. Behind came the two young guards. Slowly we moved toward Mezzegra. I kept telling Mussolini they were going to kill him, and the man outside kept insisting that he was helping him escape to Switzerland. Il Duce stared straight ahead saying nothing as if he didn't hear. Claretta held his hand, gazing at him unaware of anything else, even the gun pointing at her.

We rounded a hairpin curve and stopped outside the entrance at a villa. There was a big grilled iron gate and concrete posts on each side, a low rough stone wall with smooth coping and clipped hedge. Beyond lay a garden and the smell of wisteria. The sign read Villa Belmonte.

A curtain parted in an upper window. The frantic leader shook his pistol at it and then ordered the three of us out and up against the wall to the left of the gate, shoving us as we groped to our places. He raised his weapon. Mussolini acted dumbfounded. Claretta started crying and then screamed for the madman to stop. Through the flowering trees of an orchard across the road I caught a glimpse of the lake below—gray clouds and patches of blue sky, a few boats, shafts of sunlight on the water. Off in the distance white peaks.

The colonel began to recite a litany of the old man's war crimes and something about justice for the people, all in the name of the Volunteer Freedom Corps. It sounded like melodramatic Party rhetoric, a lot of it familiar from listening to partisans in the Second Garibaldi Brigade, and at first I thought he was reading from a pamphlet. But the guy really knew his stuff by heart. When he finished and was about to fire at the two of them not four feet away, the woman threw herself on her lover, writhing and shrieking as if to shield him. The man with the gun shouted for her to move off, and she rushed at him and tried to wrest away his gun. He pushed her back and pulled the trigger. Nothing happened. Just click, click, click. He looked dumbfounded, frightened. His hand shook. Claretta hurled herself at him again, arms flailing, fingers clawing at his raincoat and neckerchief, screaming now at the top of her voice. He pulled out a revolver, but it too failed to fire. Throwing the damn thing down, he yelled to the guard up the road and hurled her back. Mussolini stood transfixed, silent, watching with an almost blank detachment, making no move to flee or defy.

I ran up to the colonel, hollering, "Americano, Americano, Fifth Army, Como." His face twisted, his dark eyes stared wildly out of his head. He brushed me aside just as he got the new machine pistol and pointed it at the pair still with their backs against the wall. Then there was more spouting of Communist jargon. When he stopped and aimed his gun, Mussolini suddenly bared his chest and hollered something that sounded like a phrase from one of the Palazzo Venezia speeches I had seen in a newsreel. The tall man pulled the trigger and there was a terrific roar. One, two. . .nine shots. Mussolini sank to his knees and then over on his back. Claretta dropped beside him.

I watched from the gate, waiting for the gunman to turn on me. Instead he walked up to the two corpses lying side by side on the stones, blood pouring out of them, and hammered two more bullets into Il Duce's stiffening, shriveling figure. The body jerked a couple of times and was motionless. Then he turned his back on them and hurried to the black Fiat where the man in the white raincoat and the partisan who gave him the gun were waiting. Just in time too. The rain came down in a torrent.

Chapter 5

For a few minutes I remained in front of the iron gate smelling the cordite mixing with the wisteria and the damp earth, gazing after the car disappearing around the hairpin turn. The corpses stared up at me with vacant expressions—so wet, so bloody, so rigid. It was hard to remember who they were, what they had been. Harder even to realize what had just happened. Everything suddenly so quiet except for the rain beating on the red-stained cobblestones and the hedge.

The two kids left behind took out cigarettes and began to smoke, smiling, kicking the dead, poking between the stiff legs with their guns, making obscene comments. Tall, dark-haired boys wearing shabby jackets with red armbands, battered army caps, worn trousers, muddy scuffed shoes. I asked them what was going to happen now. They shrugged. They would wait until Colonel Valerio returned. Their duty was to see that no one touched the bodies. What about covering them up? They didn't understand. I went over and pulled off Claretta's coat and put it over her. They stood back and grinned.

A face appeared in an upstairs window of the villa. The boys waved their guns at it and shouted something and the curtain dropped. Then they moved back against the wall, avoiding the rivulets of blood flowing past and turning away from the corpses. Far off artillery boomed with hollow thuds.

I thought about going down to the village and finding

a car and returning to take the bodies somewhere safe. Once people learned about what had happened a mob would descend and souvenir hunters and anti-Fascists would begin carrying off whatever they could—clothing, boots, locks of hair, until nothing was left but the skeletons. Vultures picking clean the bodies.

The guards told me no, I couldn't go for a vehicle. The bodies belonged to the Italian people. That is what Colonel Valerio told them. He wanted to show them off to everybody in Milano and celebrate the end of the war, of Fascism, and of Mussolini.

The hell with that, I thought. He wanted to use them to show that the Party had won the war all by itself and returned the country to the people, to prove that Communism was now the supreme power in Italy. But it was futile to tell that to the two twenty-year-olds slouching against the wall with loaded rifles in their hands, cigarettes in their mouths, and adolescent smirks on their faces.

So I asked if it was all right if I left. They weren't going to shoot me, were they? No, no, they laughed. Americano buono, buono. I shook hands and ran down the hill to Azzano to find transportation back to Dongo before they changed their minds. There was still the treasury to locate and prevent from falling into the hands of either the Communists or the captain. At least maybe something could be salvaged from this fiasco of a mission.

Of course, that could be an empty gesture too by now, especially if the gold were already gone. I could be just endangering my life once more. The partisans could imprison me and haul me off with the Fascists they had captured to a firing squad. It would be safer to head for Como and the Fifth Army rushing up from the south. But somehow I couldn't forget that gold and the captain and what had happened to the major. Somebody had to pay for his murder, goddamn it!

It took a long time to locate a car. Most were out of petrol or wouldn't run or the owners were suspicious of me, even when I told them who I was and that the Americani would soon be there and would reimburse them. Eventually, though, I met a stumpy little old man with tiny brown eyes and a silly grin who said his brother, a butcher, lived in New York on Sullivan Street. Also he insisted that he had fought with the Fifty-second Garibaldi Brigade and was a good friend of Pedro. He would help me. He even invited me into his house to meet his wife and daughters, all shy and smiling and fat as pigs. I asked them if they had heard the news about Mussolini. Niente. I couldn't believe it. By this time I had thought everybody up and down the lake must know he had been shot.

Startled, they ran out into the street hollering about the death of Il Duce. And they urged me to come with them and explain in my best broken Italian how he and Claretta Petacci had been shot in cold blood at the Villa Belmonte. Stark silence followed my comments, then screaming, wailing, cheering, and feverish rushing around. A horde of people formed to make the journey up the hill to view the corpses. They wanted me to accompany them, treating me as a kind of hero who had brought liberation. And when I protested that I had to go to Dongo where the Fascists were prisoners, they didn't understand. Some of them, I'm sure, thought that I had killed Mussolini myself and were eager to carry me on their shoulders, invite me into their homes, cajole me to the piazza to make a speech.

"No Communista, no partigiano," I shouted. "Americano soldate." And they marched off without me, some in a jovial mood, some just curious, others looking grim. It was an odd crowd. Mostly the middle-aged and the elderly along with a few children and some teen-age girls. And for a second I debated about trailing behind to see their reaction when they encountered the corpses. But it was growing late and the rain kept falling and I felt tired. The old man looked sad. I gave him a cigarette. He smiled, and we got into his car.

It was almost five o'clock by the time we left for

Dongo. And there were obstacles all the way, partisans to argue with at roadblocks, German convoys to pass, people flooding the streets of the lakeside villages and stopping to ask if we had heard the news. At first I paused to explain what had happened, but the story aroused such excitement, provoked so many questions, so many hands fluttered in my face, I decided not to say anything after a while. And I advised Signor Perelli to do the same. He agreed, and we chugged along in his wheezing old car following the same route I had traveled yesterday. Those who had been cheering Il Duce then were now out exulting in his fall. And for some inexplicable reason I thought of Roosevelt's death a couple of weeks ago and how sad it made me feel. There was certainly no lilacs-last-in-the-dooryard-bloom feeling in these desolate little towns, no pictures or flags at half-mast, only a few grave faces.

The main square at Dongo was jammed. Along the low wall by the bay stood a line of bedraggled, frightened Fascists. Opposite them another line of partisans in fresh uniforms. Colonel Valerio stood talking to them and then arguing with several citizens. He acted as fidgety and arrogant as he had back at Mezzegra, hands waving, the long face grimacing, ranting on in that mechanical Party manner with his high voice.

Bruna's truck was parked over near the town hall, empty, the luggage removed. I looked for her and the captain. They wouldn't miss a show like this, fifteen Fascists lined up to be shot by fifteen partisans, a whole government about to be wiped out in one murderous blast. Christ, it was an even more awesome occasion than the one at the Villa Belmonte!

Then I thought of the church where Bruna had mentioned she was going to hide the cases in the truck and started out in search of it, leaving Perelli to wander among the crowd. Down the narrow streets stopping everybody I could to ask how to get to the chiesa. Nobody helped me. Some threw up their hands in disgust at my garbled Italian. Others turned their backs. A few stared and said nothing. All that seemed to be on their minds now was the momentous event about to take place in the piazza, where most of them were headed in a somber mood. One man, though, did stop long enough to say that the mayor had resigned in protest over the executions and that Pedro, head of the Fifty-second Garibaldi Brigade, opposed them. But Milano insisted that they be carried out. He wasn't going to watch them. I couldn't blame him. I wanted to get as far away as possible too.

"Have you seen any Americans?" I said. He looked at me puzzled. "Dove Americani?"

"Ah, si, si," he lit up and pointed down the street.

I ran along the cobblestones as fast as I could, shouting back, "Grazie, grazie."

And there they were all right, the captain, Carlo, and Bruno. Sitting at a table outside a cafe drinking wine and laughing. When I rushed up, they didn't appear surprised or even happy to see me.

"So you finally got your ass here, Sergeant," the captain said, leaning back in his chair. He was smoking a cigar.

"No thanks to you. That trick of putting me in the convoy almost worked. I was a prisoner for a while and might be down in the square now waiting to be shot."

"That was no trick, just a mix-up, Vic. We were going to get you out of the town hall when they transferred you. Where the hell have you been?"

"Trying to stop Mussolini's execution down the lake. If you guys had been with me, we could have taken him prisoner."

"So you were on the scene, huh? Tell us about it."

"Not now. Where's the Fascist treasury?"

"Safe and sound, don't worry."

"You guys keeping it until the army arrives? Or sneaking it out of here? If you are—"

"Never mind what we're doing. None of your business."

"It's in the church, isn't it?"

"I said, Vic, it's none of your business." He glared at me.

"Oh, yes, it is. I'm reporting it just the way I am the death of the major. You guys aren't going to get away with this any more than you are with his murder."

"The hell you say and the hell we aren't. You're not stopping us, I can tell you that. You can still join your buddies in the square, remember."

"You wouldn't do that."

"Try me." I noticed their guns on the table and resting against their chairs.

"There'd be an investigation."

"You mean a war crimes trial?"

"It could happen."

"We'll take that chance."

"I've already contacted the Fifth Army at Cernobbio. They're on their way here. You'll never get the stuff out then."

"You're bluffing, of course."

"I tried to get them to come right away. It was an advanced unit of the First Armored Division. They didn't have permission to come this far yet. They had to radio back to their commander. But they'll be here, and then you guys are kaput." I gazed around the table at the three of them. They stared back unsmiling. There was a long pause.

"What do you want?" the captain half smiled at me.

"What do you mean what do I want?"

"I mean, look do you want to give all this gold to the partisans and have it go to the Italian Communist Party or—?"

"Or have it go to you guys?"

"Right."

"What about the government of Italy?"

"That's not possible. If we don't get it out of this town, the partisans will. Take your choice. At least we're not going to be greedy, grab the whole thing. Most of it's going to the government."

"All right, let's see where the cases I brought here are

57

so I can be sure you're telling the truth."

The captain gazed around the table. Bruno and Carlo nodded. D'Alessandro stood first and they followed, picking up their weapons from the table and the ground. And we marched down the street, silent, uneasy, like pallbearers. After turning a corner and tramping down another narrow block, we came to a church. We walked in and up the center aisle. Salvatore and Giorgio were sitting on the altar with Bruna and her brother, Sten guns on their laps. The captain explained the plan to remove the five cases stacked up behind the altar. They would be taken tonight by truck to Como and handed over to the Fifth Army, that is, all but one case. It would go to Genoa where someone would be waiting to smuggle it into the States.

"What a way to leave this country and end the war, huh, Vic? Millionaires." He guffawed. So did Bruno and Carlo. Bruna and her brother looked glum. Giorgio and Salvatore didn't seem to understand what was going on. They kept smiling away enjoying the whole thing and sort of wondering why everybody else wasn't as excited as they were.

"But won't the CLNAI men from Milan search the town for the loot? They knew it was in the convoy." He admitted as much. They could come here and find everything. And they could block all roads, stop all vehicles and search for the gold. If that happened, then they would have to get the stuff out of here by boat. Enrico and Bruna had arranged for one. It would sail down the lake to Cernobbio just above Como. They would rent a truck and head for Genoa. He doubted there were any roadblocks between that area and the port city. Everything would be in too much confusion. But why Genoa? Would ships be leaving so soon for the States? The harbor had been severely bombed. It could take weeks before anything sailed. Oh, there would be some boat to Marseille. And from that point it would be easy to find a freighter going to New York. I needn't worry. He had the whole thing carefully worked out. I kept glancing at Bruna and her brother while he talked. In their brown leather jackets and rough trousers and scuffed shoes they reminded me of those scugnizzi I had seen in Naples, tough kids who knew how to steal, kill, and run. But older, shrewder, more patient.

Suddenly a priest appeared, a lean, long-faced, sad-eyed young man. He introduced himself to me as Father Bernado. Bruna and her brother greeted him familiarly. He assured us the cases would be safe. No one would know about them. We need not worry. I wondered. There was something anxious about the way he looked, acted, smiled. The captain ignored his awkwardness and said if we didn't hurry we would miss the executions in the square. He left Giorgio and Salvatore behind as guards.

When we arrived, there was Colonel Valerio still standing in front of the firing squad. The men were still practicing the ritual of execution, raising their sub-machine guns and aiming to fire while he recited the orders in precise terms and the commander of the group repeated his words verbatim. They were the only sounds in that crowded hushed area. The victims who hadn't turned their backs yet, stared vacant-eyed at the people and the muzzles in front of them, hands and ankles tied, waiting for the signal to face the bay and their fate. Some seemed barely able to stand, looking pale and shaky. Others looked resigned, shoulders slumped, expressions solemn.

I recognized a few from OSS descriptions that I had read of the men in Mussolini's Salò Republican government—Mezzasoma, Minister of Popular Culture with thick glasses, a wiry little guy twitching and turning; Pavolini, Party secretary, even more malevolent than I had imagined with that mustache and white face, standing on one leg most of the time and grimacing. The others, middle-aged, heavy, bowed down, acted like a group of derelicts who had been hauled into a police lineup for identification. One, much younger than the others and in the military, smoked a cigarette and

59

smiled at the death squad in bravado fashion.

It was hard to believe the thing was actually happening. Like a scene from a movie with hundreds of extras. Shooting Mussolini and his mistress was one thing. They seemed somehow to be fulfilling a tragic destiny. But these cowering, mangy sad sacks stretched out in front of me from the public urinal south along the low wall with the fishing jetty and the lake in the background and the mountains beyond didn't seem ready to die. Why they hadn't tried to escape like a number of others in the convoy I couldn't figure out. All morning people had been drifting away from the line and disappearing into Musso. But there they were, the men who once ruled the country, now gaunt ghosts of a vanished power.

The crowd grew tense. Some sobbed, a few cried out in protest. There was one anxious moment when two shots rang out from a window and the whole squad turned and fired a blast at the building. After that incident a profound silence settled over the piazza broken only by the clicking of guns, muffled weeping and muttering, the hoarse voice of Valerio going through the execution ritual again and again. Then just as the commander was about to give the signal to fire for the second time, the colonel chewed him out once more. It reminded me of the pistols that didn't go off at the Villa Belmonte—the same playacting, the same petty attention to detail in the face of death, the same utter absurdity of men waiting to be shot and the squad ready to fire and the mustached martinet in the brown raincoat turning the screw tighter and tighter.

I slipped away without anybody noticing, edging through the spectators. The expressions on their faces grew tauter the longer they waited for the firing to commence. Eyes focused on the scene with an intensity that I had never seen before, hundreds of men and women and even a few children transfixed at the horror about to burst upon them. The suspense mounted, the hush deepened.

After what seemed like a long deep breath there were cries of "Viva l'Italia" from the victims as the gunfire exploded. Not just a couple of shots or one fusillade but round after round banging, slamming, tearing into the bodies along the wall. Then a moment of sudden quiet as the echo of the gunfire reverberated through the town and faded out over the water. Another one of those intense hushes followed by screaming, wailing, cheering.

I hurried along the street hunting for the church. Giorgio and Salvatore were still sitting on the altar. I told them that the captain wanted the cases put in the parish house. People would be coming from the square after the executions and saying prayers for the dead. They nodded and together we lugged each one through the side door to the house next door. The priest came in and helped us. We had to hurry because already there were footsteps outside and the sound of voices. And just as we finished carrying out the last heavy case, several women entered and started up the aisle. He left us to greet them.

"Padre," I said just before he turned away, "I'll be back in a little while with the captain and Bruna and her brother."

"Si, si," he muttered and dashed off to meet his parishioners, the vigil candles flickering in the twilight atmosphere.

I went into the kitchen at the back of the rectory and covered up the cases with newspapers and told Giorgio and Salvatore to take care of the gold. Although I had no clear idea at that moment of what to do or how I was going to get the stuff out of here by myself, I knew I had to come up with a plan soon to frustrate D'Alessandro and at the same time save my own skin. He was no more going to turn over any of this treasury to the Fifth Army than the Commies were. It was just a game to see who could outwit whom.

Outside darkness was falling fast. I hurried along the narrow street, keeping my eyes on the stones. Most of the people going by were silent, the only noise their shoes scraping the pavement and ringing through the dusk. They looked like shadows climbing a wall. Upon reaching the piazza, I stopped and viewed the bodies laid out on the ground. Sixteen of them. Signor Pellici saw me and said that Claretta Petacci's brother had just been shot trying to escape into the lake. He had been masquerading as a Spanish diplomat and was exposed when someone spoke to him in Spanish and he couldn't respond. His small wet corpse lay alongside the others.

The captain, Carlo, and Bruno stood gazing at the dead and talking to the men in the firing squad. Puddles of blood were everywhere. Contorted, masklike faces. A sickening odor filled the air. I felt like vomiting, and it took a moment to get my stomach and nerves under control.

"Where did you go?" D'Alessandro came up to me.

"I had to take a leak."

"Too much for you, huh? You missed a great show, the death of an era."

"I saw my historical moment flicker a little while ago at Mezzegra."

He lowered his voice. "We'll wait till they get these damn stinking things out of here before we bring the cases to the boat. I guess we better not try the road. Already this Colonel Valerio is asking about the gold and instructing his men to be on the lookout for it. He suspects something. But I don't think Enrico or his sister will talk. We got them scared shitless. The lake should be misty by ten. We'll load up then. Now let's get back to the cafe and have something to eat and do a little celebrating."

I said I wasn't hungry and would meet him at the church around ten.

"You going to stay to help load the corpses for their last journey?"

"Where are they taking them?"

"To Milan along with Mussolini. The Piazzale Loreto where the Krauts killed fifteen people last year in

62

reprisal for a partisan bombing. They call it Piazzale dei Quindici Martiri now. It'll be a real homecoming for the old bastard. That's where he started you know, in '22. Who the hell says you can't go home again?'' He guffawed. I walked away, thinking about the fact that I was born that same year.

After a couple of turns around the area watching people leave and trying to get someone to talk to me, I came back to the bodies. A yellow furniture truck pulled up and Valerio and the men of the firing squad began loading the dead. It was a tedious process, lifting the blood-soaked stiffs and arranging them in order along one side of the interior. I went over and watched, staying out of the colonel's way. He didn't recognize me even when his eyes turned in my direction. He was too busy talking about how upset the mayor, Pedro, and the people were over the executions, some of them swearing to return and get revenge. All the time cursing, gesticulating, smoking one "Oriental" cigarette after another. When the last corpse was packed in, he barked out orders, and he and his men piled into a black Lancia Aprilia and a brown Alfa Romeo Spider and sped off. Two guards stood at the rear of the truck ready to hop aboard and join the carcasses.

I walked over and told them that I was an Americano and wanted a ride to Milano to report to the Fifth Army. They scrutinized me for a minute, not saying anything, two short, wiry types in military jackets. All of a sudden one started to raise his machine gun, and I yanked out my .45 and got the drop on them both. They froze. I waved my arm and told them to beat it, get out of the square as fast as they could or I would shoot their balls off, gesturing to the streets behind the town hall. They turned and ran, and I fired over their heads.

The driver and his friend came running around from the cab, pistols in hand. I yelled for them to drop their guns. They did, a puzzled, terrified look on their faces that reminded me of the expressions on the men they had just killed not more than an hour ago. One of them,

63

a short, sharp-faced guy in his twenties, small hands, long hair, sweater, suddenly smiled at me. His name was Giuseppe. His friend was Mario, taller, thinner, quieter, wearing a cloth jacket. He didn't smile. I told them to drive me to the church nearby. They shook their heads, complaining that they didn't know where it was. I would direct them. All they had to do was to follow my signals.

So we closed the rear door and went forward to the cab and climbed in. For a minute there was silence. Then they wanted to know if I was going to bring the bodies to the church. No, the priest was hiding the gold taken from Mussolini, and we were going to take it to Milan. I was working with the CLNAI. The two guards who ran away thought I was a spy. Besides, I heard them talking about selling the bodies and stealing the Fascist treasury for themselves. I had to get rid of them.

Giuseppe shook his head. Mario gazed off into space. But the lorry started and we were on our way to the church through the darkness. Headlights lit up the deserted square. An eerie pall seemed to be descending on the whole town and the lake and the hills beyond. I knew this was one place I never wanted to come back to if I could help it.

Chapter 6

Father Bernado was eating supper in the kitchen with Giorgio and Salvatore when I entered the parish house. He said that the captain had been looking for me. And I told him I had just seen him and he sent me here to pick up the cases. I had a truck outside ready to load. Instead of taking the treasury by boat to Como as planned I and two partisans were driving it in a van.

He acted skeptical. So did Giorgio and Salvatore. The captain never told them anything like that. And for a moment as I studied the three of them I wondered what to do next. The priest wrinkled his brow, set his mouth, brooded on the stone floor. The two kids frowned at me, Sten guns on the chairs. But when I invited them outside to view the truck, they suddenly changed their minds and agreed to help me carry out the gold.

Before I opened the rear door of the lorry, however, I warned them about the bodies piled up along the right side. They were the Fascists executed in the piazza this evening. The smell was very bad. And they shouldn't take a look if they had weak stomachs. There was a lot of blood. The captain wanted to use the vehicle so no one would suspect what we were carrying, thinking it was just the Fascists. Thus nobody would stop us, search us. The driver had an official CLNAI pass and wasn't aware of what we were up to.

Grimacing and crossing himself, the priest stepped back from the truck and then ran into the parish house followed by Salvatore and Giorgio. I went after them to explain the situation further. But now the three of them somehow seemed scared, especially the father, of the whole business and wanted no more to do with me or the cases. And the priest wanted nothing more to do with the partisans, muttering something about the slaughter of innocent people, men taking God's justice into their own hands and becoming murderers. It was no use to talk to him. His face took on a melancholy cast. He didn't look too well somehow. And I kind of wondered if all this business was not only depressing him but somehow undermining both his spirit and his health.

So I left him sitting by himself in his study watched over by a large crucifix and two holy paintings and a couple of small statues. Salvatore and Giorgio went back to their supper. How long it would be before the captain arrived and discovered the hoax I didn't know. Maybe I had a half hour, maybe even an hour's head start.

Before climbing back into the truck and starting the journey down the lake, Giuseppe and Mario wanted to open the cases and see the gold. But we didn't have time. Possibly we could stop somewhere along the way. Now we had to get the hell out of there fast.

I explained to them as we started to roll that our story would be a simple one. We were transporting the dead Fascist gerarchi to Milano on orders of the CLNAI. Didn't they have passes? They showed me them, yellow pieces of paper stamped with a red star authorizing them to travel in the area in the name of the Volunteer Freedom Corps. The cases contained Salò Republic documents. As for me, I was too ill to talk. If worst came to worst and we had to enter into a fire fight, I thought we had enough weapons to run any roadblock, shoot up any barrier. The main thing I wanted to impress upon them was that they should remember the corpses belonged to the Italian people and we were taking them to Milano to show them to the people. A new Italia was rising out of the ashes of the old. Viva l'Italia!

Giuseppe acted impressed with the scheme and my rhetoric despite my crude Italian. He started to talk as if the whole thing were a lark, puffing on one homemade gray-looking cigarette after another. Mario appeared quieter, a little hesitant to agree with me about what we were doing, still worried about the two partisans I had chased away and about carrying so much gold in the same truck with the dead.

The two of them said they were from Turin and had gone to high school but never graduated. They were Communisti, at least they insisted they were and wore the Red star on their caps. But they didn't spout the Party line or appear to be anti-American or anti-British like so many I had met up there. Each had dozens of friends and relatives killed in the last couple of years, some by Tedeschi, some by Fascists, some by Allied bombings. Still, it seemed to me, despite the losses and all their hardships and deprivations they enjoyed the war. In one way it was like playing hooky. In another way it had given them what they apparently had never known, a purpose and a passion for living.

We careened through the darkened streets of the little towns strung out along the lake, nearly running down dim figures walking or riding on bikes. Splashing, roaring, lighting up doorways and green shutters, the rain slanting down in the headlights and the wipers slapping away and the puddles jumping. Giuseppe kept up a cheery chatter while working the wheel, Mario telling him constantly to slow down and watch for this hole and that turn. I sat between them silent, listening to the cases sliding around in the back, wondering what was happening to the bodies.

Mario didn't want to stop at Mezzegra for Mussolini. It was bad luck to transport him. His spirit could seize possession of us, drive us to destruction, cause some terrible accident. Giuseppe told him he was pazzo as we rode through Musso and on to Menaggio. Nobody had stopped us yet. He pointed out that without Mussolini in Milano there would be no celebration. His body had to be there for everyone to see that Fascism was finished forever. If Mario didn't want to ride with us, he could get out and walk. The tall, thin kid turned and sulked, gazing out the window and didn't say another word.

We hit the first checkpoint south of Menaggio, lanterns swinging across the road and partisans shouting at us. In the distance the sound of gunfire. The Fifth Army must have been mopping up the last remnants of a German force. Giuseppe stopped and pulled out first his yellow Red-star pass and then a white one. Looking closely at the second in the guard's lamp, I saw the signature of Captain Silvio from OSS, who must now be in Milan. He was supposed to meet the major there and help him with the CLNAI liaison work as well as contact the Germans in the surrender deal Dulles was arranging. Mario, too, showed both of his passes. They claimed that I was from Dongo and assisting them. The dead in the back were Fascists executed this afternoon. The partisans took a quick look, but nobody jumped in to inspect the bodies. The stench was too strong, and they laughed about our riding to Milano breathing Fascist shit.

While we were halted and sipping some coffee, I got out and glanced back up the road. Any moment I expected to see a car or truck come roaring out of the darkness carrying the captain and his crew. But so far no sign of them. And very little traffic. Just in case they did show I told Giuseppe to instruct the guards to detain the American capitano. He wanted to take the corpses away from us and bring them to Rome, hand them over to the Allies. He didn't want the Italian people in the North to see those who had brought so much shame to the country. He translated the message, and then we jumped aboard and were off for the hills and Il Duce.

Since the road up to Mezzegra was too narrow for the van, we had to stop and rent a car. It took about an hour locating one. Finally we found a Fiat 1500 and went racing up after the dead, at least Giuseppe and I did. Mario stayed behind to guard the truck.

68

The scene at the villa was just as I had left it, the two guards leaning against the wall, the wet, blood-encrusted corpses lying on the cobblestones side by side. Only Claretta's mink coat and high heels were missing along with one of Mussolini's boots. The whole place felt creepy with the rain coming down and the odor of damp flesh hanging heavy in the air.

We went over and talked to the partisans and told them who we were and where we were going and what we wanted. They acted skeptical. Colonel Valerio had warned them he was returning for the bodies and to surrender them to no one else. But after I slipped each kid a few thousand lire, they agreed to release the dead pair and even rode down the hill with us to the truck. Then they insisted that we take them to Milan. I said fine, but they would have to ride in back with the stench. There was no room up front. And if they did ride back there, they took the chance of becoming sick. After taking one whiff of the morgue on wheels, they decided to stay where they were.

As we left them, they acted kind of sad, standing by the side of the road waving listlessly, their great moment fading. Never once complaining of the rain and the cold that they had been enduring for hours. Somehow I felt we had deprived them of a poignant experience and wished we could have taken them along. Then I thought, hell, I gave them a lot of lire. That's all they really cared about. Only I was a sucker for the great moment bit.

The closer we came to Como the closer the war seemed once more. Star shells and tracers filling the sky. Explosions thundering through the hills. Roadblocks more frequent and the partisans manning them more belligerent. Each time we stopped it seemed they searched the truck more thoroughly, asked more questions. But no one opened any of the cases, taking our word that they contained documents and not lingering long amid all that carrion. Mostly what they wanted was a good look at Mussolini and his mistress. And after that a hasty glance around was sufficient to satisfy their curiosity.

It was fascinating to watch them view the body, first the excitement, then the hostility, finally the awe. Peering with big eyes and smiling, cursing, spitting, making the sign of the cross. Some demanded souvenirs and tried to tear a piece from his trousers or shirt, cut slices of leather from his boot, clip hair from Claretta. And if we hadn't been there they might have dismembered the ghastly lovers. But after the first few minutes most just stared silently, maybe wondering what it all meant, Il Duce gone and everything he did and stood for finished.

Festivities livened the villages we passed through—bonfires, music, dancing in the square. Communist slogans splashed across the walls of buildings over faded Fascist phrases. Red flags hanging from balconies. Pictures of Il Duce defaced and torn. Drunken shouting and wild cheering. From windows the flickering of candles and the sound of voices singing. It was as if the whole country were on holiday and letting go.

And as we drove through the gauntlet of local celebrations, uneasy, wary, watching for a challenge to stop, we began to feel more conspiratorial than ever. Wishing we could avoid every barrier, every curiosity-seeker, every Communist. More aware of the gold we carried than the bodies. Scared someone would discover it and hold us up and run off with half a billion dollars. Several partisans did come close to opening the cases. And once we actually had to stop at gunpoint. If our secret got out, we would lose everything, the cases, the bodies, our lives. We could be accused of stealing the country's wealth.

At Como we ran out of petrol. It was eleven o'clock. Still no Americans in the area although there was plenty of gunfire in the outskirts and a lot of rumors concerning their movements. The people told Giuseppe that the Fifth Army was just a few miles southeast of the town and should arrive at any moment. I thought about waiting for them, but he and Mario said no, they would go out and find benzina. They had to be in Milano tomorrow morning. Colonel Valerio was expecting them. He would shoot them both if they didn't appear, which meant that somewhere along the road I had to take off with the cases and hide them until I found some Americans. And that would be difficult with the two of them watching me like cats.

Just as we started from a side street onto Viale Varese I spotted the captain and the gang cruising around in a Fiat minus Bruna and her brother. Moving slowly, stopping people and asking questions, shining flashlights in doorways.

I warned Giuseppe that the Americans I had told him about were hunting for us. It would be hard now to leave the city without being seen. We'd have to quickly find a safe place to park the truck out of sight, wait a couple of hours, and then make a break for it.

Luckily, Mario spotted an empty garage, and we backed in at the right time. For just as we were pulling down the door, the Fiat with the captain driving turned the corner and headed in our direction. It passed by. They hadn't seen us. Or had they? After a few minutes they came back, slowly this time, poking along, shining lights into every building. I grabbed a Sten gun out of the cab. So did Giuseppe and Mario. If they entered the drive, we would flip open the garage door and fire right into the middle of them.

A damp oil smell rose from the cement floor. We crouched on each side of the van, Giuseppe and Mario on the left and I on the right. Listening. One heave on the door and we would start pulling the triggers.

Five minutes passed. Nothing happened. The car kept roving back and forth, back and forth, stopping, starting, turning and shining headlights into the drive. At last it halted. The motor turned off. Footsteps scraped against the pavement. I found a side door and slid out noiselessly, hugging the wall. The man walking out there silhouetted against the building was the

71

captain, still dressed in uniform, still wearing paratroop boots, carrying a carbine. I could have hit him easily from my spot provided the damn gun didn't jam.

Back and forth, back and forth he strolled as if trying to guess where the hell the lorry had vanished. He halted right in front of the garage and yelled down the street.

I melted back into the building, shuffled over to Giuseppe and Mario and told them to get ready. Americani were coming after us. On my signal we would throw up the overhead door and rush out and surprise them, guns popping. They no doubt would block the entrance way. It would be risky. Five against three. And they were heavily armed.

Mario grabbed me from behind and whispered that he had something. I turned around, and he pressed a grenade in my hand. I whispered, "Grazie, grazie, buono, molto buono," and slipped out the side. Salvatore and Giorgio were now standing in front of the Fiat blocking the drive, the small headlights illuminating the garage door. They had Sten guns. Perfect targets. I couldn't understand it. Why were they exposing themselves that way if they suspected we were in here? And where was the captain?

After pausing a moment, I tossed the grenade overhand in their direction. Like a throw from the outfield to home plate. A terrific explosion ricocheted off the wall. The lights went out. The car exploded into flames. Giuseppe and Mario slipped out and started firing rapid bursts. Then a sudden silence, as if someone had blown a whistle. The only sound the flames licking the ruins of the car in front of us. No sign of the two partisans. Down the street footsteps running.

We walked out to view the smoking remains. Although I was becoming used to dead bodies, the sight of Giorgio and Salvatore blown to bits by the blast, their limbs and torsos burned black almost beyond recognition, was sickening. Pieces of flesh scattered everywhere along with blood and hair. I dry-retched a couple of times. Giuseppe and Mario stood impassive in

72

the glow of the dying fire and then went back and brought out the truck. I jumped in and we were off again, roaring into the street past the smouldering hulk of the Fiat and the burned corpses, glass crackling beneath the tires, the strong smell of rubber burning. No sign of anybody. We turned left just in case and headed toward the outskirts searching for signs to Milano.

We didn't go very far when there they stood at the corner waiting for us, the captain, Bruno, and Carlo. Positioned in the center of the street, guns ready. They saw us. No backing up or stopping now, no turning around. Instead Giuseppe bore down hard on the accelerator, and we balled right through the intersection going sixty, bullets pinging and zinging and rattling against the sides of the lorry, the glass on the right door shattering.

But we made it intact with only a couple of side windows broken. Giuseppe gave out a cry, Mario sat silent. I kept glancing back. No traffic at all. Far off the crackle of gunfire and the thump of shells bursting. We were moving into the country beyond Como now, out into the hills. Still no American units appeared anywhere. The only people around were peasants and partisans and a few German soldiers walking forlornly along the road. In less than an hour or so we should be coming within sight of Milan.

"Molto fortunato, no?" I said to break the tension of the cab.

"Si, si, fortunato," Giuseppe echoed me. But he wondered about the next time. He didn't think Americani would give up that easily. The closer we approached the city the rougher would be the inspections of the furniture lorry. Someone was bound to discover the gold. Maybe the rumor we were carrying it along with the bodies had gotten out. A band of partisans or Fascists or even Christian Democrats could ambush us.

The thing to do, then, I tried to impress on him, was

ditch the truck at the next town and transfer the cargo to another lorry. No, he objected, that would be too difficult. It would require too much time, create too much suspicion. What if we hid the cases somewhere along the route and came back for them later? That didn't work either. He was afraid Colonel Valerio would think we were tricking him. And he was sure the Colonel would be waiting for us and know all about the gold. Someone in Dongo probably had found out about our theft and telephoned CLNAI headquarters in Milano. If we didn't arrive with il tesoro, we could all be shot. And I thought of Bruna and her brother. They weren't with the captain in Como. They certainly could be suspicious of me since I had told Bruna that I wanted the gold for the Allies.

So we drove on, trusting to our luck and hoping we could reach the city before all hell broke loose.

And it looked as if we were going to succeed. Giuseppe had found a back road, wild and desolate and no sound of war anywhere. It was after one. The rain had slackened and the mist was thinning out. We had the whole rolling countryside to ourselves. There wasn't even a house in sight, only mountains.

I asked Giuseppe what he thought was going to happen next to prevent us from reaching Milan in time for the victory celebration.

"Foraturao, boom, boom," he laughed, slapping me on the arm.

And no sooner had he spoken and touched me when the back wheel went bump, bump, bump, and we pulled over on the shoulder, turned off the headlights and looked around and didn't say anything. Slowly the stink of the dead flesh seeped into the cab so you could almost taste the stuff, feel it crawling over you like a chilly slime. And the country around us so eerie, so quiet, so dark. Not a light anywhere. Not even a single star.

74

Chapter 7

We were stuck out in the middle of nowhere—no jack, no pump to blow up a soft spare, no house nearby, no traffic. Giuseppe said we would have to wait until daylight for someone to come along. Which would delay the fireworks in Milano all right, the dance macabre around the corpses and the frenzied crowd, the rabble-rousing speeches and the big Red machine roaring into high gear. I could envisage a wrecker towing us into an empty Piazzale Loreto by late afternoon and people on the sidewalk laughing at the crippled yellow van and wondering who would be moving on Sunday and where was that terrible stench emanating from. What did we have in there anyway, a dead whale?

"Ah, si, we go," Giuseppe exclaimed. "Okay, okay?" Impatient, he started the truck. I protested. The wheel wouldn't last half a mile if we drove on the flat. The lorry would be permanently disabled. And then I thought of the cases. There would be no chance to hide them at all. Lost to the Allies and Italy forever. The entire Pontiac mission down the drain, everything I had risked my life for so far kaput. Christ, no!

Mario remained silent through the dilemma, watching, listening, acting as if he were waiting for something to happen. Giuseppe told him to get out and go find someone to help us. Reluctantly, he opened the cab door and started off across a vacant field toward a clump of trees, acting sullen and not saying a word. After he had gone a couple of hundred yards, lights flashed ahead down the road. We yelled for him to hurry back. He came running as we dashed out to the middle of the pavement and started waving our arms frantically.

It was a charcoal-burning car with a potbelly stove in the rear chugging along at about fifteen miles per hour, the burnt damp smell fouling the air. The driver stopped and got out. He was a wizened little old man in a sheepskin and Alpine hat but no Red star or armband. A thin, wrinkled woman and two scrawny kids peered out the windows.

Giuseppe talked to him. Yes, he had a jack and an air pump and would help us. We told him that we were partigiani going to Milano. The war was finito. Mussolini had been executed. There was going to be a victory celebration this morning. He smiled and, becoming excited at the news, suddenly embraced each one of us.

"Americano," I introduced myself, shaking hands and then proceeding to the car and reaching in and greeting the woman and the kids, patting the heads of the shy girl and the big-eyed little boy. The three of them remained huddled inside gaping at me as if I were a person from another planet.

Mario and Giuseppe found the jack and the pump and got to work raising the truck and pulling off the right rear wheel. Then we all took turns pumping up the spare, even the old man. After we had finished, he wanted to know what we were transporting. The smell was so bad.

Giuseppe laughed and turned to me.

"Tell him," I said. After all it was the least we could do to repay him for his help. "What the hell! Open the back up. Let them all have a peek at the great man and his woman and the gerarchi. It would be an experience they would remember for the rest of their lives."

So Giuseppe described in Italian what we were hauling. He got excited again and went over to tell the news to his family. They emerged from the car and stood at the rear of the truck with him, waiting for us to unlock the morgue on wheels. He held the flashlight we used in changing the tire. And as soon as the doors opened he shone the beam into the black interior. The woman gasped, the eyes of the kids bulged. The old man threw up his hands and shouted in a piercing voice. "Diavolo, diavolo!" And he ran to the car followed by the others. They piled into the jalopy and drove away in the direction that they had come.

"No buono, no buono," Giuseppe said. Mario looked worried. And I could read their minds. Roadblocks springing up and die-hard Fascists ambushing us and demanding the bodies and the cases. Still I couldn't believe that anybody would accept his story. And at this time of night who would be awake? Where would he find an audience? But they insisted that he would arouse his friends in the nearest village and spread the word fast. In no time the entire highway between here and Milano could be swarming with angry peasants, police, soldiers, partisans, souvenir hunters, Fascists. And we would be at their mercy.

So we jumped in the truck and raced after the charcoal-burning car, its rear red lights fading into the night and fumes hanging in the damp air. As we passed it, I poked the Sten gun out the window at the dumb bastard, motioning him to pull over and stop, when Giuseppe yelled, "Villaggio, villaggio!" Up ahead on a hill loomed a cluster of stone houses with a few candles flickering in the windows.

We bumped over the cobblestones in second gear, the motor reverberating through the hollow spaces between buildings. Balconies, green shutters, narrow doorways. A fountain in front of the town hall splashed away. A belfry stood out against the sky. Darkened shops and a cafe with the metal shutters down. No sign of anybody. Then down the hill and onto the flat again. The old man in the charcoal burner had disappeared from view as if swallowed up by the night. Giuseppe pressed his foot down harder on the accelerator, and we spurted forward. The truck jerked and my gun fell to the floor.

"What are you doing?" I yelled at him.

"Look, look," he said, pointing to the rear. I glanced back, and there were two cars racing toward us and gaining rapidly, small and fast with tiny headlights.

"Partigiani?" I said as the wind flowed through the cab.

"Polizia," Mario muttered.

"Fascisti?"

"No, no," Giuseppe answered. "Fascisti finito. Carabinieri."

Swinging around a sharp curve, he cut off the light and the motor and coasted into a clump of trees. The Fiats zipped past. Uniforms inside, guns pointing out the windows. After a couple of miles they would turn and come searching for us. We couldn't stay here or go back. Either we abandoned the truck or put up a fight.

Giuseppe eased back onto the highway in low gear, lights still off, groping along. No sound of motors returning. The first side road we hit we turned and shot down the rough pavement, switching on the lights and squealing around curves. It was hillier and narrower and eventually became dirt. If this were a dead end, we would never make Milan, that was for sure. But the road kept on unraveling and we kept on bouncing around. The only trouble wsa that we weren't headed in the right direction as far as I could tell. North instead of southeast.

Another small town thrust up out of the landscape. Another old car poked along in front of us. Then a cart and a mule appeared with a lantern swinging between the rear wheels and a man asleep on straw rocking away. He never stirred as we whisked by. And I couldn't get out of my mind the bodies sliding around in back amid the cases and the flat tire. Every now and then a deadly odor swept through the cab.

There was no more traffic until we came to the east-west highway to Milano. The sign read 20 KM. And suddenly things felt easier. Except the closer we moved toward the city the less chance there was to dump the cases off somewhere without Giuseppe and Mario knowing. And I was faced with the prospect once more of seeing everything I had risked my life for go down the drain. Of course, I could force them to stop and get out and then drive off. But in no time the CLNAI would be on my tail. And I didn't know the country around here. Or I could shoot them. But, no, cold blood was not my style somehow. At least I didn't think I had reached that point yet.

Few vehicles were moving through the early-morning darkness, but each one we passed aroused suspicion. The captain and his crew could be hiding somewhere along here waiting for us. The police and the partisans too. After all it was the main highway, and they knew this would be the only way we would be coming to the city.

A barrier loomed ahead. Two lorries were parked across the road hood to hood with a gap between. Shadowy figures stood in front of them, armed. Already I could see in the headlights their hands going up, guns thrusting at us.

"Go through?" I asked.

"Stop and we go through, no?" Giuseppe snapped back.

"Buono." He aimed for the gap between the two trucks and came to an abrupt halt a couple of feet away. Our lights shone through the opening into the darkness and the silence beyond. Partisans swarmed around us, guns drawn.

Giuseppe protested that we were under orders from the CLNAI to proceed to Milano. He showed his two passes. So did Mario. But this time it didn't work. They demanded to inspect the truck. At first Giuseppe refused, then he said he would let them see Mussolini and the Fascists if they would let us go through immediately. We had to have the bodies at the Piazzale Loreto by three A.M., and it was already after two.

The news of what we were transporting caused a

79

sensation. The men laughed, threw up their hands, a few even fired their rifles into the air, all acting like kids after their team had won the homecoming game. Was the war really finito? Giuseppe got out and took them around to the back, asked for a flashlight, and, after opening the big rusty doors, lit up the interior. At first all the bodies looked alike scattered everywhere, and the men kept yelling, "Il Duce, Il Duce! Dove Il Duce?" Fearing somebody might enter the truck, I jumped up and dragged him by his feet forward to the tailgate. The corpse was still wet and caked with dirt and blood and stank worse than ever. Heavy as lead too. Someone yelled he couldn't see very well. So I lifted the old boy by the shoulders and propped him up until he stood like a scarecrow. A hush descended as the familiar figure in the militia uniform minus one jackboot and riddled with bullets rose over the ragged group of partisans—black shirt, gray-green tunic, striped pants, the great shaven head. The group shrank back. I explained that it took nine shots to kill him, the last one in his heart. He was executed by a Communist at Mezzegra near Lake Como.

"Morte ai Fascisti!" a voice shouted and a clenched fist went up.

"Libertà ai popoli," another voice answered with another clenched fist. A partisan started to climb on the tailgate. I put down the body and shoved him off and then lugged the carcass back into the darkness. I brought Claretta forward and propped her up in the same manner. Laughter exploded. Obscenities peppered the atmosphere. Hands reached up to touch her shoes, her skirt, and I could detect a gleeful sensuality in their eyes as they gazed up at the doll-like paramour—the oval face, the white blouse, the corduroy skirt. Quickly, I drew her body back into the interior, threw a canvas over it, and jumped down. Giuseppe locked the door. We faced the circle hollering, "No more, no more," waving our hands. They raised their rifles as if to challenge us. Giuseppe and Mario protested their inno-

80

cence. And I realized that they weren't going to come to my rescue. They weren't even going to prevent the partisans from shooting me to get at the gold if it ever came to that. They owed me nothing. Besides, before they were Red or enemies of Fascism or anything else they were Italians and they would use that face against me in a pinch.

"Tedeschi, Tedeschi!" I cried, pointing behind the men to a vehicle approaching at a high speed with headlights burning brightly. Everybody scattered. I pulled Giuseppe and Mario with me to the cab and told them to get in and drive like hell out of here. It could be the Americani we saw in Como.

Giuseppe gunned the motor and rammed between the two vehicles in front of us with a thunderous crash. After a momentary stall, like a fullback driving into a line and being stopped by a hand, we broke into the clear and leaped forward. Bullets hammered away at us. The Fiat had halted at the barrier. Then we lost it and the lights as we roared around a turn. But on another straightaway there it appeared again bearing down on us faster and faster. I thought about stopping and tossing out the cases and letting Giuseppe and Mario go on to the city without me. They could tell Colonel Valerio that the Fascist treasure had been taken off and hidden to prevent capture. And he would have to believe them, that was all. But how would I ever find transportation for five heavy cases? And there wouldn't be time to bury them even if I had a shovel. Yet I had to do something. It wasn't far to the outskirts now. And once we reached the city there would be no chance to stop and escape with the loot.

"Slow down," I yelled above the noise of the motor. "Let them get close. Do we have any more grenades? Bomba a mano, bomba a mano?" Mario reached down and handed me one.

The car came up fast now spraying the back of the truck with round after round. Giuseppe moved into the opposite lane so whoever it was would have to pass on my side. As soon as I saw the headlights even with our rear, I opened the door, holding it with my left hand. When the vehicle edged forward, I hurled the thing as hard as I could just as a fusillade hit the truck with tremendous force. There was an explosion, a fire, and then another explosion. No more headlights or gunfire. Just flames and muffled firecracker-like noises fading farther and farther behind us as we sped on toward Milan.

"Okay," I shouted in the cab, "buono okay." But who it was we had blown sky high I wasn't sure. It could have been the police, partisans, Fascists, even the captain. The main thing was we had breathing space. A sign read, "Milano 8KM".

Now all I had to do was figure out how to prevent the gold from falling into Red hands. I thought of Captain Silvio who had signed the passes and remembered reading in a message to the major that he would meet us at the Hotel Milano, temporary OSS headquarters. Why not go there first and pick him up, tell him about the gold, and then let him decide what to do? Giuseppe said no. We had to head straight for Piazzale Loreto. Colonel Valerio was expecting us. He would be angry.

So the best thing to do, I thought, was to forget the whole thing, give up the mission, ask Giuseppe to drop me off before we reached the city. After all, I had done everything I could. My conscience was clear. Why risk my life anymore? Hell, it wasn't my money just as this wasn't my country. In a couple of months I would be out of there for good and everything would be a memory. Nothing is permanent in war anyway except for the dead and why end up among them now at my age? My turn would come.

The truck sputtered, kicked forward a couple of times, started to run smooth, then stopped in the middle of the road. The engine cut off.

"Motor?" I said.

"Benzina." I looked at the gauge. The needle was at empty. Either we had sprung a leak or used up the gas put in at Como with all the running around on the back roads. We got out and pushed the lorry to the shoulder. There couldn't be more than five or six kilometers left to go. We must be on the outskirts. So I told Giuseppe and Mario to take a couple of cans and go off and steal or buy or beg some petrol. And I gave them each a handful of lire. I'd stay and guard the truck.

It wasn't as desolate as the last place we stopped. A cluster of houses stood close by—lights, some tall buildings in the distance that looked like warehouses and factories. To the right an abandoned stone structure with windows boarded up and no door, just an opening.

As soon as I got the two cans from the back and Giuseppe and Mario disappeared with them, I walked over to investigate the place. At one time it probably had been used as a shop or storage shed. One story. No machinery or furniture inside, boxes or bags. Nothing except old newspapers and the smell of urine. Not a very safe place to stow the cases. But stumbling around, I discovered a couple of loose boards and under them a large hole that seemed wide and deep enough for the entire load.

So I hurried back to the lorry and one by one dragged the cases into the building and pushed them into the pit. Then I nailed the boards down with my shoe. And none too soon. Giuseppe and Mario returned more quickly than I had anticipated with four cans of petrol found in the back of an abandoned German truck down the road.

The two of them were in a jovial mood, laughing away, delighted with their discovery. In another hour we should be at Loreto. It was three o'clock. Late but at least we would make it before dawn.

They poured the gas into the tank and we started on the last leg of the trip. The drizzle had stopped. A chilling breeze blew through the truck. Still it wasn't strong enough to dissipate the decaying damp smell of the corpses. The air felt heavier and heavier with their odor. When I took a deep breath, a sickening sensation swept through me, and I had to squeeze hard to prevent myself from vomiting.

Giuseppe saw me struggling and pointed to the window. I shook my head. I was all right. He and Mario started laughing. Each gave me a pat on the back. And just as we entered the city, I did open the door, lean out, and let go. We slowed up, and I kept on heaving, leaning out over the stones. I wondered if I was ever going to make it to the square.

Chapter 8

The nearer we approached to the heart of the city and the Duomo, the Galleria, and La Scala, the scarier the scene. At first just a few deserted streets, darkened buildings, isolated lights, sporadic traffic. Then a distant machine gun chattering away, a shell bursting, a flare lighting the sky over some rooftops, the ping, ping of rifle fire. We passed a truck on fire and heard nearby the roar of a truck.

We darted down a silent side street, parked in front of a group of shops, their metal shutters rolled shut.

I proposed that we head away from the center of the city and come at the piazzale from the north instead of trying to dodge our way through streets where we might encounter fighting. It was already late. Three-thirty. But we couldn't worry about that now. The main thing was to deliver the goods and get the hell out of there.

"Okay, bene, bene," Giuseppe said. And we rolled down to the corner and turned right when a lorry pulled up in front of us and a dozen figures leaped out and started firing. Giuseppe cut the lights and the motor and Mario and I shot back. But we didn't have a chance to get off more than a couple of rounds when the attackers swarmed over the running boards, shining lights in our faces, ordering us to surrender. They were urban partisans, men in their twenties and thirties, wiry, tough, excited, dressed in threadbare coats, voices high, waving rifles and Sten guns and machine pistols like sticks.

We climbed out of the cab, protesting we were under orders from the CLNAI. Giuseppe mentioned General Cadorna and Luigi Longo. But nobody paid any attention to what we were saying. Even my announcement that I was an American didn't impress them. They frisked us hard, took away my Sten and .45, Giuseppe's beretta, Mario's pistol and knife. What did we have in the truck? We told them and a couple of the men went around with the keys and opened the doors and peered in. They ran back to proclaim that we were Fascists on our way to bury Il Duce and his gerarchi. We should be shot immediately and our bodies turned over to the partisan command. I held out my dog tags to prove my identity. No one understood them nor could they grasp my crude Italian. And Giuseppe and Mario didn't try to defend me or explain my situation. Instead they struggled to make clear their own identities, pointing to their papers, the red stars on their caps.

"Non capisco," the leader kept saying over and over, a big truck driver type wielding a Sten gun. He shoved me toward a wall between two shops, shouting, "Fascisti, Fascisti." We stumbled backwards, lights now shining in our faces blinding us temporarily. Except for the brightness it was like Dongo and Mezzegra all over again.

I thought about explaining what happened to the gold to distract them. At least it would delay the executions. But no, that would only convince them further that we were Fascists. The best thing was to send someone to Colonel Valerio at the Piazzale Loreto. And I told Giuseppe to explain that to them. He did and they refused to believe him. None of them had ever heard of the colonel or knew where General Cadorna or Luigi Longo could be found. We were just stalling.

Standing against the wall, our feet and hands bound, we faced six of them aiming their rifles and machine guns from a couple of paces away. The headlights of the truck blinded us. Nobody was even going through the ritual of reading out our crimes. We were going to be shot down like stray dogs.

Giuseppe knelt on the cobblestones, his back to the guns. Mario turned around too. I stood facing the partisans, no blindfold on, blinking at the lights and trying to see the figures. We waited. The leader watched us as if extracting from the situation every bit of melodramatic suspense he could, starting to give the signal to fire and then hesitating. And I thought of the machine pistol that had jammed on Valerio when he pointed it at Mussolini, of the story Dostoevsky told about lining up to be shot and seeing the hair of the man beside him go white, his whole life pass before his eyes, eternity flashing by in a few seconds.

Mario muttered to himself. Giuseppe wept. My legs weakened, and a terrible pain gnawed at the pit of my stomach. I bowed my head no longer able to look at the light or the guns, wishing like hell that there was something to hold in my hand—a picture, a crucifix, a ball, anything to squeeze to keep the pressure inside from bursting. My mouth felt terribly dry. A thin stream of urine trickled down my leg and burned.

A shot rang out, then another and another. Giuseppe moaned. Mario muttered prayers. I was sure my hair was turning white waiting for the bullets to hit. Nothing happened. Round after round chipping away at the stone wall over my head. Suddenly everything stopped.

The big man with the Sten gun and Stalin-like mustache approached guffawing in a bluff hearty way. I tried to smile, but my lips were too numb as if full of novocain. My body felt paralyzed. I leaned back against the wall drained, ready to collapse. Beside me Giuseppe had his head on the stones kissing the pavement. Mario stood immobile, silent, his back to the squad. A partisan came over and untied us and handed out cigarettes. It took two men to pull Giuseppe to his feet and hold him upright, his legs buckling each time he tried to stand alone. He could hardly hold the cigarette in his mouth much less light it. Mario smoked unsteadily. I took a couple of quick puffs, my fingers fumbling, watching the firing squad enjoying our discomfort and wishing I had a gun to mow them down.

"Perchè?" I said into the air. "No Facisti. Partigiani. Il Duce a Piazzale Loreto. Capisce?" They looked at me smiling. The leader scrutinized us, his Sten gun at his side. A rough, blunt face, big hands, small eyes, a bushy mustache, a cigarette dangling from his mouth.

"No gold?" he said in English.

"Parla Inglese?"

"Un po'. My mamma, my papa, they go to America before the war. I stay, fight Fascisti, Tedeschi. Buono, no?"

"Communista?"

"Ah, si. Buono, no?" He gave the clenched salute.

"Molto buono," I said, putting out my hand to shake with him. "I am Italiano too. Victor Del Greco."

"No gold?" he repeated, ignoring my hand. "We know Il Duce have molto, molto tesoro."

"Somebody else must have gotten it, or it's back in Dongo. We have only the bodies. You help us get to Piazzale Loreto? Colonel Valerio is waiting for us. He's the one who shot Mussolini and the Fascisti in Dongo. He told us to bring the bodies here."

"Okay, buono, we take you. We give you a flag to show. Nobody stop you."

"A Red Cross flag?"

He laughed. "No, no, Red flag. Communista."

"The Communisti running the city?"

"Ah, si, all Nord Italia now Communista—Turin, Balzano, Venice, Milano. Tedeschi e Fascisti finito. Guerra finita."

"What about the Fifth Army?"

"No come."

"OSS? Do you know if Captain Silvio is at the Milano Hotel?"

"He came to Hotel Regina first and see SS, Colonel Rauff. Americani e Tedeschi very good friends, no?" He laughed. "You friends with Fascisti?"

"No."

"Communista?"

"No."

"Communisti rule Milano. Some day we rule Italia. Okay?"

I didn't argue with him and quickly changed the subject, asking if he wouldn't help us to get to Piazzale Loreto right away. We were already an hour late. He told us to hop into the truck. He would ride in front with Giuseppe and me. Mario would go in the other lorry. Two partisans jumped on the running board with rifles ready, one of them inserting a Red flag in the grill.

"I thought you said you guys controlled the city. Why the protection?"

"We make sure you go to Loreto. No one stop you. Tedeschi, Fascisti are hiding. They have weapons."

And it did sound as if the enemy were still around, though not very active—sporadic gunfire, an isolated explosion, a flare lighting up the night sky. Just enough war to make you nervous driving through the darkened streets. At one corner there was a battle going on between one group in a building and another outside crouching behind a barrier. A short machine gun burst and an occasional grenade. We stopped and turned around and went up another way searching for a quieter passage.

"Did you know we were coming?" I asked the tall mustached partisan squeezing between Giuseppe at the wheel and me scrunched against the door. The more I studied the big muscular man the more certain I was that he had been in the Spanish Civil War. He reminded me somehow of so many Communist veterans I had met in OSS. They all had that same easy confidence about them as well as a kind of fierce inner intensity—playfulness mixed with an obsessive drive. So different from Colonel Valerio at Dongo and his frantic racing around, his emotional speeches.

"Si, I hear. Molti rumors Mussolini dead, gerarchi shot, a lorry bringing them to Milano."

"You hear about the gold, too?"

89

"Molto oro. You no see it?"

"No," I looked over at Giuseppe. "Maybe Colonel Valerio brought it in his car. He gets the perfume, we get the garbage." I laughed.

"After all these years I like the smell of garbage better than the perfume of gold."

We both lapsed into silence, watching the headlights shining on the tram lines and the wet cobblestones, listening to gunfire coming in waves from different parts of the city. Since no stop lights were working and there was little traffic, it didn't take long to drive into the black square and park at an abandoned gasoline station. Overhead loomed the girders and cement beams of an unfinished building. They looked like a huge spiderweb against the sky. Just in front of us stood an Alfa Romeo. Colonel Valerio and another man got out and walked toward us. Their footsteps resounded through the stillness of the empty square.

We stepped forward to greet them. Valerio, still wearing his raincoat, beret, and neckerchief, hollered out something in Italian, and I knew by the tone of his voice it had to do with our being late. I didn't glance at him as we approached, only at the other man beside him— taller, sharper head, longer arms, thinner shoulders. He was Colonel Gentile. There was a sinister sort of self-assurance about his posture so different from the frenetic energy of Valerio. He shook hands firmly and measured me a long time before speaking.

"Il Duce?" he said unexpectedly in a low hard voice that was more military than Party. I pointed to the rear. And we walked around to the back of the truck. Giuseppe unlocked the door. The colonel gave a crisp command and two men behind us jumped out of the shadows and into the interior.

The unloading of the corpses proceeded quickly. The men flashed their lights around searching for the dead, and then handed down each one to Giuseppi, Mario, and me. We dumped them on the pavement in a circle. There were eighteen all together. Somehow just touching a cold hand repelled me in a way that I didn't think possible anymore. I could be numb to the business. Still the clammy skin, the dried blood, the stiff hair combined with the dampness and the stench and the mud on the uniforms got to me. And I was relieved when we finished with the last body.

The two colonels and the mustached partisan leader ambled among the dead shining lights on each face. Every one was distorted in some way—a mouth twisted, an eye socket vacant, bullet holes in a cheek or forehead, a chin broken, skin discolored. I never thought human beings could look so inhuman.

When the three of them arrived at the body of Mussolini, the heavyset guy pulled out his pecker and squirted the famous face and laughed. A few others came up from behind and imitated him. The colonels watched, not saying anything.

What a weird homecoming for the old guy, I kept thinking. Lying here at four in the morning in a skeleton gas station reeking of urine and putrefaction and looking like a piece of decayed wood that would crumble if you kicked it. And not twenty-four hours ago he had been moving through those little Lake Como towns strutting his stuff. Standing by his Alfa Romeo, hands on hips, chin out, surveying the crowd admiring him, only a touch of resignation in that baggy face. And Claretta adoring from a distance in her mink coat and high heels—the black hair, the dark eyes, coquettish smile, big breasts. Christ, it didn't seem possible that they were gone and I was still there and the war was almost over, a war that at times I didn't think would ever end!

"The gold," Colonel Gentile snarled at me. "Bring out the cases." He turned and gave a command in Italian to the two men still up in the truck.

They disappeared into the interior again with their lights. I moved close to Guiseppe. Everybody clustered around the tailgate, the tall colonel in the middle flanked by Valerio and the burly partisan leader. For a

91

second, I thought about running like hell. Up one of the five streets converging on the square from every direction. No lights anywhere. It would be better to beat it and take my chances than face an inquisition and another firing squad.

A couple of minutes passed. Nothing happened. Gentile yelled into the truck, his voice rising and quavering. The two men continued rummaging around making a racket, poking their lights into every corner. Finally, they came to the tailgate for brighter lights and plunged back into the deeper darkness still reeking of the dead bodies. Sweat poured off me despite the cold air and misty drizzle falling.

Giuseppe turned in my direction, and though I couldn't see the expression on his face, I could visualize it. One of his hands grabbed mine tight.

The men came to the opening again, shrugging their shoulders, putting out empty hands. "Niente, niente," they shouted together. Everybody stood motionless staring at them.

Chapter 9

Colonel Gentile jumped onto the tailgate and shined his light around, then turned and spouted something to the partisans, who grabbed the three of us and jammed guns into our backs. He accused us of stealing the gold and demanded that we tell him where we hid it. If we refused, his men would kill us on the spot. We would join the dirty Fascist dogs on the cobblestones. His tone of voice and position on the rear of the truck waving the flashlight around made him seem like a towering, terrifying Old Testament figure looming over us.

"La, la," Guiseppe kept shouting and pointing, indicating that if he looked under the canvas he would find the cases. The Colonel disappeared into the cave-like area again and this time came back holding up a covering. Giuseppe and Mario turned on me, protesting their innocence and insisting that if anyone took the gold I was the one.

"Okay, okay, all right, si, I took it," I confessed. "They had nothing to do with it."

"You take our gold," the big mustached partisan stepped toward me, poking his Sten gun into my ribs. Valerio stood beside him spitting something out in his nervous intense way that I couldn't grasp. Guns clicked at ready. I was sure they were going to kill me right then and there.

"But it's not yours," I protested. "It doesn't belong to the Communist Party. It belongs to the Allies, to Italy."

"To the people," Gentile said. He jumped down. Valerio covered me with a machine pistol, the same one I was sure that had killed Il Duce, jabbing it closer and closer until the muzzle was under my chin. His breath smelled hot and sour. Gentile moved closer. The metal scraped my skin. I touched the spot and felt blood.

"You tell us, Americano," Gentile spoke in that brusque, gritty, gravelly voice of his. "We give you one, two, three momenti."

"Okay, okay, si, capisco."

"Dove, dove?" he said.

"Outside the city. On the route we came in on. Giuseppe can show you. I don't know the name of the road or remember exactly the place. But it's on the Como highway. Where we stopped for petrol." I gazed around to check on Giuseppe and Mario to see if they recalled and would come forth with the information. They stood staring at me neither understanding nor wanting to.

"You show us," Gentile barked. "Subito." He pushed me toward the cab of the truck. Giuseppe would drive. The man with the Stalin mustache would sit in front with me. Mario and the others would ride in back. He would follow in the Alfa Romeo. Colonel Valerio would go and report everything to General Cadorna in the Palazzo Cusani.

"What if the Fifth Army gets here in the meantime looking for the Fascist treasury?"

"You tell Americani where you hide gold?" Gentile bore into me.

"What do you think? My orders were to capture Mussolini and take charge of the treasury from Lake Garda."

"No, it belong to Italian people, not capitalists. To Italia, not America. You do not own us because you fight in our country."

"Yeah, but don't forget it's our war too, Colonel, and you were once the enemy."

The three of us climbed into the cab and Giuseppe

started the motor. It sputtered and stopped. He threw up his hands. "No benzina, no benzina!" The partisan called back to Colonel Gentile just about to get in the sedan. He stalked over, a revolver in hand, and for a moment I thought surely he was going to blast me out of my seat. Instead he said for us to wait right there. He would go and fetch some benzina.

"No gas, no gold," I said outloud to myself, sitting between Giuseppe and the partisan. Neither of them cracked a smile or said a word. The only sound was the Alfa Romeo thundering across the piazzale and disappearing down one of the five streets entering the square.

The big man squeezed in beside me, opened the door and started to get out.

"What's the matter?" I said.

"Cigarette. You have one, no?"

I reached in my pocket, watching carefully the Sten gun he fingered on his lap. As he leaned toward me to grab the pack he assumed I was going to produce, I hit him in the neck with the blade of my right hand, a hard swift stroke like the swipe of a knife. He choked, doubled over, and I whacked him again, this time on the nape as fiercely as I could. There was a low gurgle and then a silent slump in my lap along with blood drooling from his mouth. Limp.

Giuseppe uttered a muffled cry, and I whirled around and clamped a fist on his mouth. He jerked back.

"Stay here. I'll take care of the two in back with Mario."

And I untangled myself from the slack body, crawled over him, and slid out the door, taking his Sten gun. Whether he was merely out cold or dead it was impossible to tell. But I thought the last blow had severed something and he was gone for good. He felt stiff.

Around back the two partisans were talking very loud. I approached quietly, one step at a time until I reached the tailgate.

A light rain continued to fall. A light breeze blew. It was a cold, wet spring night that seemed more like March than April. Buildings surrounding the square stood out tall and dark and thick like fortresses. Overhead the girders resembled gallows. And the bodies on the pavement looked like so many sacks. Gazing around, I took in the square, vast and eerie and full of foreboding. Like a barren stage in an empty theater. Even our voices seemed to resound. I kept waiting for someone to turn on the lights and for an audience to appear out of nowhere. Off in the distance the dull roar of guns and explosions.

"Tedeschi, Tedeschi!" I hollered, revealing myself in the opening. The two partisans ran out to the tailgate, Mario behind them. They had guns. I sprayed them with the Sten. The chatter was deafening, bounding and rebounding against the stone buildings. They each fell with a jump to the cobblestones. Then a second of silence. Mario jumped down.

"Giuseppe," I called.

"No buono, Victor, no buono," he ran up and saw the bodies. "They kill us. You give them gold. I fear."

"Don't worry, the Allies will protect us."

"No, no, Communisti kill us. I know. You, too, Mario. They find gold. Finito, finito. No buono, Victor, no buono."

"If we can find Captain Silvio he'll help us. The Fifth Army will be here soon. They'll stop the fighting and put down the Communists. They won't dare touch us or take over the country. You'll see."

"Si, si, they came back." He looked at me. Mario stood behind him speechless as usual, taking it all in with that inscrutable blankness. I patted Giuseppe on the shoulder and told him to follow. Mario too.

"We go find gold?"

"No, no, Hotel Milano, Captain Silvio. Remember the yellow paper you have. He signed it. He's in charge of the whole city for the Allies until the troops come. Capisce?"

He remembered, and I went on to explain that we could lead him and some American soldiers to the hiding place of the Dongo treasure. It was in a small building right at the spot where we had stopped for petrol. I hid the cases under the floorboards.

Neither of them said a word or seemed to be listening. They were staring down at the two dead partisans on the cobblestones. I could read their thoughts: *too late, Americano, too late. We are Italiani. We stay and you go home. They shoot us. You have lire and live far, far away. We help you, but you cannot help us.*

"Okay, let's get the hell out of here," I ordered and ran across the open space in the opposite direction from the one the Alfa Romeo took a couple of minutes ago. At first they stayed behind and I was out there alone pumping hard and never thinking I would reach the safety of a building. Then Giuseppe and Mario started up, their footsteps scraping behind me. Any moment I expected bullets to come flying and a spotlight to pop on.

A car entered the piazzale behind me. I stopped and looked back. It parked beside the van and the two figures got out and stood for a couple of seconds surveying the scene before jumping back in and zooming off.

"Chi è?" I asked Giuseppe as he caught up with me.

"Colonel Gentile. He go to see General Cadorna. Everybody in Milano look for us. They say we have gold. No buono, Victor."

"The Fifth Army will be here tomorrow. Don't worry. We can hide out until then."

"Partigiani find us. I know."

"We'll go see Captain Silvio first. He'll protect us. We'll tell him where the gold is and he can go get it himself."

"CLNAI demand OSS give it up. They lose molti, molti lire. The Party is strong in Milano, Victor. I know. We ride with Colonel Valerio to Dongo. He talk about gold, not Il Duce. That is what he want, that is

what the Party want. Molti, molti lire. Il Duce è cacca."
He spat.

"Maybe you're right. Maybe they'll even try to strike a deal with Silvio if they haven't already. If he signed your pass, he must have signed one to let Valerio go to Dongo to execute Mussolini. We'll just have to assume he's on our side. Anyway it's better than sitting in the van, isn't it, and waiting for them to shoot our balls off?"

"Si, it is better now. Later I do not know. We lose lire and our life, no?"

"You know where the Hotel Milano is?"

"Ah, si. Via Manzoni."

We turned and walked fast through cavernous streets —black, damp, creepy, guns still crackling in the distance. Close to four-thirty. Every time a car or a figure came toward us we scurried into a doorway and squatted down. The whole city seemed ghostly, few lights or vehicles. Bombed-out buildings looming through the darkness. The rain falling harder and harder and the silence deepening. It felt as if the entire population had deserted or gone underground.

"Duomo," Giuseppe said, pointing ahead to a massive marble structure etched against the night sky. We entered the huge piazza in front, passed through the Galleria, and came upon another tremendous square. "Teatro alla Scala," Giuseppe muttered. "I show you Tedeschi." Suddenly we were going past the Hotel Regina, sandbagged, machine guns sticking out of a couple of windows. "SS," he whispered. The place was dark.

"Tedeschi gone, no?"

"Possible," he said.

"Where the hell's the Milano?"

"It is not far. We go. Via Manzoni."

All of a sudden there was an American flag flying from a fourth-story balcony, a dim light on it. Looking forlorn on that long desolate street. Nostalgia welled up inside me. It was the first Stars and Stripes I had seen in weeks except for the patches we wore on our parkas when we parachuted on Mount Mottarone in February. I started to run toward the hotel. Giuseppe grabbed me.

"Captain Silvio, Americano," I shouted at him, breaking away.

"Gentile know you come. He wait. Boom, boom, boom. No buono."

We ducked in a doorway and watched the hotel entrance down the block. A couple of empty cars sat parked along the curb. No guard around. A few lights burned in the rooms on the ground floor and above, including the one with the flag flying from the balcony. We waited. And we waited. Not a soul anywhere.

"We can't stay here till it gets light." I nudged the two of them. "We've got to try and get in there somehow and see the captain. Gentile wouldn't dare attack us in the open."

"He capture you. You are only one who know about gold. He make you talk. When he have tesoro, finito, amico, finito. You kill partigiani." And he drew a hand across his throat.

"What'll we do then?"

"I go."

"But they know you too."

"I find amico. He know if Americani in hotel." He pointed to the balcony with the flag. "He come, tell us. Okay?"

He slipped off down the street away from the hotel. The sky was beginning to lighten. The rain had stopped. It still felt cold and damp, though, cold and damp and deserted. Gunfire continued to bang and crackle and boom in the distance. Sunday morning. And I thought how nice it would be to go to the Duomo after a long sleep and a breakfast of bacon and eggs. My stomach rumbled at the thought. It had been almost a day since I'd had anything solid and five days since a regular meal.

"Victor," Giuseppe whispered from down the block. Two figures darted into the doorway. "Angelo," he introduced a little guy in a sweater and cap. "He say Americani in hotel. He deliver message to them from CLNAI. Multi partigiani in lobby. They wait for you with Colonel Gentile. They shoot you, Victor. Non buono."

"Can he get a note to Captain Silvio?"

"Si."

And yet, I thought, suppose he is intercepted. That would make matters worse. The thing to do was to go up to Silvio's room myself and hide until the Fifth Army arrived. And they should be in the city at least by tomorrow.

"Can he get us inside the hotel without our going through the lobby?"

"Si, he know way. He know room Americani stay. No soldati in Milano. All partigiani. Tedeschi, Fascisti finito. Everybody go to Piazzale Loreto di buon mattino. Communisti control Milano, Nord Italia."

It took us over fifteen minutes to dart in and out of doorways—down long streets and through cluttered alleys—to reach the rear of the Milano. Mario and Giuseppe knocked out the guard and tied him up without any trouble. We rushed in and up the back stairs to the fourth floor and along a wide, high-ceilinged corridor that reminded me of a palace. Angelo pointed out the room, and I rapped on the door. No answer. I rapped harder, more insistent. Still no one stirred.

"Sergeant Del Greco, Pontiac mission," I said. "For Christ's sake hurry up and let me in. The bastards are after us."

The door opened, and I walked into a lighted, well-furnished sitting room where a captain and a lieutenant stood in OD's and paratroop boots, .45's on their web belts.

"Jesus, I thought you guys were at Como picking up Il Duce. That's the last message we got."

"We were supposed to grab him, but things haven't turned out too good. Major MacGregor's dead.

100

Possibly Captain D'Alessandro too by now, Carlo and Bruno. But I'm still alive and kicking, at least for the time being.''

Silvio was a stocky, swarthy man with curly hair, a trim mustache, a genial handshake, a boyish kind of enthusiasm. A typical OSS officer. The guy with him, Lieutenant Barbatti, was thinner and taller wih slitty eyes and a strange way of staring and making you feel uncomfortable.

"You were at Lake Como, weren't you?"

"That's right at Dongo and Mezzagra. Mussolini's been shot. So have most of his ministers. I was there. The bodies are at the Piazzale Loreto on public display this morning. It's going to be a real orgy.''

"So they got him. I was supposed to take him back to Caserta. Corvo said you guys would capture him at Como and then the First Division would bring him here. He was sending a plane to the Bresso Airport not far from here.''

"The Commies were determined to do the job themselves and not let the Allies take the credit. I tried to stop them. It didn't work.''

"You?"

"I even brought the bodies all the way from Lake Como in a furniture van.''

"Holy Christ!''

"Giuseppe and Mario here helped me. This is Angelo, who got us into the hotel through the back door. The Reds are guarding the lobby looking for us. You see we brought not only bodies to the city but the Fascist treasury too and hid it. They say it's worth half a billion.''

"Whew! Where did you hide it?"

"Outside of town on the Como road. They tried to force me to tell them where, but I got away and they're hot on my tail. We had to take care of a few of their joes, and they might want revenge.''

"That's not good, Del Greco. We just had a show-down with the partisan command over the Germans in

101

town. They want to massacre all of them and we're trying to arrange a peaceful surrender with Colonel Rauff at the Regina. But this Fascist treasury business is another thing. They could be up in a minute when they find out you're here."

"And they'll find out pretty quick when they discover the guard we took care of."

"Christ! General Crittenberger and the Fifth Army haven't arrived yet. Only Major Rosselli from AMG and a lieutenant. They're at the Gallia on the Piazza Duca d'Aosta. Came in yesterday ahead of the army. They thought the city had been occupied."

"It is occupied all right, by partisans, and they're running wild shooting up the place."

"That's why we can't just go out of here and pick up this Fascist treasury you're talking about. They'd be sure to seize it and us too."

"And kill us in the process. But I'm afraid somebody will discover where we hid the stuff if we don't do something fast."

"Can you give me a rough idea of the spot where you hid it?" I tried, but he shook his head. "I'm afraid I'll have to show you, sir."

"Okay, I'll call Rosselli and see what he says. He's the one who should take care of the money for the Allies anyway."

"Then I bet it ends up in the hands of the Communists."

"Well, all we can do is try to see that it doesn't. Half a billion. Wow, Del Greco, do you know I wouldn't mind having a couple of thousand of that." He smiled. "All in cash?" I told him that from what I had heard the treasury consisted of in addition to lire, gold bullion, wedding rings collected during the Ethiopian War, foreign currency, jewelry, and securities.

"And you say they're down in the lobby laying for you?"

"I think a Colonel Gentile. We gave him the slip at Loreto, but Angelo says he's camped out down there waiting for us. And when he finds the guard's been taken care of he'll be up here fast."

"Well, I've kept the lid on so far pretty good."

"Yeah, but, Captain, you didn't have half a billion they wanted. They could bring an army up here and take us without much trouble. I saw how they treated Il Duce and the Fascists. No trial or nothing. Just bang, bang, bang, and it was over. These guys are out to seize power in a hurry anyway they can before they lose the advantage."

"You better beat it then. Hide somewhere. Crittenberger will be here soon. And once the IV corps arrives they won't dare touch you. If they do, we'll blow the fuckers off the map. That's one thing these guys understand, firepower."

"You're not going to hand over the gold to them, are you?"

"What the hell do you think? Not if I can help it. But if it comes down to our survival I am. My job here is to arrange a surrender with the Germans, and all I've got is a flag outside and a couple of carbines and the two .45's. Besides, it's not our money, it's not really our affair."

"But it's our war, Captain," I said. "We've lost a hell of a lot of men getting rid of Fascism for them, maybe not as many as they did, but damn near it. Major MacGregor's death was pretty horrible." I filled him in on the details. He sat listening, shaking his head, gasping as I bore down on the blood and the gore.

A knock on the door. We froze. Giuseppe and I moved toward the next room. Silvio motioned for us to stand still.

"Colonel   Gentile.   Committee   Nationale Liberazione."

"What do you want?"

"General Cadorna send me to talk to you."

"Domani. I'm sleeping."

"Subito."

"No, domani."

"We talk to you, Capitano."

"We've already gone over Colonel Rauff's situation at the Regina. As soon as the Fifth Army arrives, they'll surrender."

"We not talk about him. We want Americano with you. The Fascisti, Giuseppe and Mario. We know they are there."

"Sorry. They're in my custody. I can't release them."

"We come in."

"You do and I'll put a hole through your damn thick skull, Colonel."

"They steal Fascist gold, Capitano. It belong to the Italian people. General Cadorna say we arrest you if you do not give them to us. Capisce?"

"You mean if I don't give them and the gold to the Communist Party, don't you, Colonel?"

"No, no, to the Italian people," he said in that deadly, decisive, harsh tone of his.

"I'm going to have to hand you over temporarily, Del Greco," he turned to me and whispered. "Sorry. It could create a bad incident. We could lose contact with the CLNAI, and they could start a bloody massacre of Germans and Fascists in this city."

"But they'll kill us," I stared at him. "After they force us to tell them where the stuff is hidden, it's kaput. You can't do that. We went through hell to bring it this far. You can't let them take us, sacrifice us like this. Jesus, the damn war is over!"

"Okay, Del Greco, you win."

"Capitano, we come subito. You hear me?"

"Capisco, capisco," Silvio said. "One momento. I'll open up. Del Greco has agreed to come out to keep the peace. But you've got to promise not to harm him."

"We want gold, Capitano. We no harm Americano. He tell us where it is and we let him go. No harm. Americani amici."

Silvio waved his lieutenant to one side of the room and the four of us to the other. We took out revolvers. The instant he opened the door we were to begin firing with everything we had. He paused while we got in position. Then he put his hand on the knob, jerked hard, and stepped to his left. No one was there. A blank corridor.

"Where the hell are you, Colonel?"

"Down the hall. Send Americano and Fascisti. No shoot. Amici, amici. Okay?"

Silvio walked out into the hall and turned right. We waited with our guns still out and ready. He came back.

"It's no good. The place is swarming with the bastards. All with machine guns too. We could be dead in a minute. I'm afraid we're going to have to let them have their stinking gold. I don't think they'll touch you, Del Greco. They want good relations with us. They need food and medical supplies and money. And we've got an army coming."

"No," I said, "you're wrong. They'll kill us. They're not going to let anybody live who knows about the gold. The only way maybe we have a chance is for you to go along with us to the site. They're not going to kill you too, the senior American officer in Milan. It could go hard against them."

"So now you say let them have the Fascist treasury?"

"Not exactly. Let's all go to the place where I hid the stuff and make a deal. It's risky. They could get carried away when they see the gold and shoot us anyway. But it's worth a try. Get Rosselli in on it too. They'd think twice about shooting you and him both."

"Right now you mean?"

"Sure, why not?"

"But I can't leave here, Del Greco. I'm in charge of the whole city for the Allies until Crittenberger arrives. You go. I really don't think they'll harm you. Just scare you."

"You guarantee that?"

"Definitely. Any harm comes to you, I'll blow the whistle on them. And they understand that. Rosselli will back me."

"Well, I guess we don't have much of a choice then.

But tell them we keep our weapons, and we ride in separate cars. Mention that you talked to Rosselli on the phone and he knows about what's going on and who and where we are. Better call him and tell him to come with us. That'll even the odds. Shooting a major is a lot different from shooting an enlisted man in civilian clothes.''

He went out the door and down the hall once again and came back to tell us that the colonel agreed to my suggestions, even to including Rosselli. There would be a car outside the hotel in about ten minutes.

Fine, but what about some rest first. All of us except Angelo had been going full-steam for almost forty-eight hours straight. A guard could remain outside the door to make sure we didn't escape.

Gentile grudgingly consented to give us two hours. He and his men had to be at the Piazzale Loreto by eight o'clock. So the captain closed the door and Giuseppe and Mario took the chairs and I flopped down on the couch. Angelo preferred, he said, the floor. As we dropped off to sleep, the last thing I heard was Silvio and Barbatti whispering in a corner. The sky was beginning to turn from black to gray.

Chapter 10

Suddenly I woke up and daylight was streaming into the room, horns and sirens were sounding, church bells were ringing. I walked out to the balcony, and, my God, hundreds of people were flooding the street below shouting and waving, hugging and kissing each other. Cars and bicycles everywhere.

Silvio and Barbatti had left along with Angelo. I shook Giuseppe and told him to go ask the guard in the hall what was happening. He returned with the news that everybody had heard about Mussolini and the Fascists and were off to the Piazzale Loreto to see the bodies and celebrate. The war was over. A new age was beginning. No more Fascism, no more oppression. Liberazione.

"Did you ask him about room service?" I quipped. Ignoring me, he indicated we were to hurry and get dressed and go downstairs to eat breakfast in the main dining room.

So we trooped into the lobby with the partisans behind us, and there stood the colonel smiling away and looking so different from last night—clean-shaven, a fresh shirt, shiny shoes, in an ebullient mood that contrasted starkly with the sullen grimaces and sharp commands of a couple of hours ago. He had a car outside and was eager to take us to Major Rosselli at the Hotel Gallia. We had to ride with him and his men on account of the traffic. We would never get through unless we did. He even suggested that maybe we were right and the

Fascist treasury should be turned over to the Allies until a new government was established in Rome.

"You received new instructions from the Party?" I grinned.

"We work together, no? It is much better. Everybody happy."

"No Red state up here," I continued to grin at him, searching for some flaw in that long, thin, ascetic face.

"No Red state. Everybody happy."

We gulped down the eggs and the coffee and stale bread and rushed outside to the green Alfa Romeo that resembled the one I had seen Mussolini riding in from Como to Dongo, the same silver and ivory steering wheel and luxurious interior. A Red flag stuck out from the hood. He got in front with the driver. Mario, Giuseppe, and I slumped down in back. And we were off in the direction of the Statione and the Piazza Duca d'Aosta.

The streets were so packed that the guards had to jump off and walk ahead to clear a path with their guns. And at other times we got stuck in the traffic and had to sit there prisoners of the multitudes swarming throughout the city on this joyous, unholy Sunday. I couldn't imagine anybody going to mass, although lots of people were pouring out of the churches. It seemed as if most of the population were joining in the festivities, moving aimlessly, jubilantly, making as much noise as they could. Red flags flying all over the place. The names of Stalin and Lenin smeared on buildings.

The sights were incredible—the headless corpse of a German soldier propped against a post with a Chianti bottle stuck in his neck, civilian bodies littering the sidewalks like carrion on the highway and pedestrians stepping over or kicking them, shaven women herded along down the middle of the street with a hammer and sickle painted in red on their foreheads and spectators spitting and jeering and dashing up and striking them. Communist signs and banners everywhere. Weapons flashing in the sun, pistols, rifles, machine guns. On one corner a disabled German tank with Red slogans scribbled across the sides in blood-dripping paint. Drunks and dancers and even some people dressed up as Indians prancing around and whooping.

At the Hotel Gallia we stayed in the car while the colonel ran in to fetch Major Rosselli. He was a short, bald man with a little tidy mustache, sensuous mouth, pudgy hands, abrupt movements. Very dapper, very excitable. He wanted to go to the Piazzale Loreto before we headed for the gold. And he and Gentile stood on the sidewalk arguing about it, their hands shaking as if they were haggling.

While they were gesturing and sounding off and everybody was watching, I thought about bolting and disappearing into the crowd milling around in a festive mood. But the guards remained by the car with their guns ready, occasionally glancing at us. Nothing would give them more pleasure on this Sunday than to shoot the nuts off an American Fascista.

The major won the argument and crammed into the back seat with us, Gentile in front. The guards leaped on the running boards to ride shotgun. And we were off for the big Red orgy.

"So you're Sergeant Del Greco," Rosselli turned to me, "the one who brought Il Duce and his gang here last night. Captain Silvio told me about it over the phone. Good work."

"Right, sir. Giuseppe and Mario helped." I introduced them. "It was a rough ride."

"And you hid the gold? Didn't trust the partisans, huh? Over half a billion the captain told me."

"I hope it's still safe. It'll mean a lot for the next government."

"Christ, just look at this mob, will you? Too bad you couldn't have taken the old bastard prisoner. But then, of course, we wouldn't have this spectacle. Boy, these people are saying goodbye to Il Duce with a bang all right."

He gazed out over the throngs as we crept through the

109

congested streets stopping and starting, blowing and threatening to run people over if they didn't get out of the way. The closer we came to the Piazzale Loreto the bigger and more enthusiastic the crowd became. It was like a Times Square New Year's Eve party. Clusters of partisans sprouting Red stars and waving Red flags walking along arm in arm singing. Fireworks popping off. Guns firing in the air.

"We do not stay long, Major," Gentile turned around and addressed us. "We get gold subito, okay?"

"Oh, sure. I just want a quick look. It's going to be something to write home about. You don't see anything like this more than once in your lifetime."

A mass of humanity jammed the open space where the five streets converged. Thousands were surging around the unfinished gasoline station, screaming, chanting, spitting, raising fists at the corpses hanging by their ankles from the girders like so many carcasses in a meat locker. Trousers and shirts torn. Claretta's corduroy skirt tucked between her legs and secured by a belt, her white blouse ripped to expose her petticoat and breasts. Her face smeared with blood and dirt, and pieces of her baby-blue underpants showing. Mussolini stretched out and dangling upside down in his red and black striped trousers, a jackboot on his left leg, mouth and eyes hanging open to the ground, his face bruised and bloated and livid with red and purple marks. Like a man reversed on the Cross. A horrifying sight when I thought of seeing him alive only yesterday. The jaw broken. His uniform tattered. Yet for all the grotesqueness and ugliness the whole sight was exhilarating, almost electrifying with everybody pumped up in a holiday mood. One woman next to me explained how she had thrown mud on Il Duce before he was strung up. Another had fired two shots into his body for the two sons she lost in the Ethiopian War. And another boasted of kicking and trampling on his body.

Gentile stood behind us on the fringe of the crowd, looking nervously around. Rosselli wanted to move closer, pick up a souvenir or two. Giuseppe smiled and shouted with the others, caught up in the madness of the moment. Even Mario, usually so dour and silent, was gesticulating and shouting. I thought of escape. But the guards kept eyeing us, guns at ready. Still it wouldn't have been difficult to take off. They wouldn't have dared to fire into so many people. There'd be a panic. But even if I managed to get away for a moment, in the end they'd catch up with me. So I just watched and waited for the dapper little major to satisfy his curiosity about the horror show.

"Sergeant, isn't this tremendous?" he beamed at me, his small black eyes glittering. "Ever see anything like it? This is the way all wars should end, the men who started them strung up in front of the public that had to endure them. Too bad they were shot at Lake Como. They should have been lynched right here before everybody. What a glorious Sunday morning!"

"I saw them die, Major. It wasn't so glorious. It made me sick to my stomach if you want to know. Something I never want to witness again."

"I know how you feel, son. And maybe in a way it would have been better if you had captured them alive and we flew them to Caserta. That's what your boss, General Donovan, wanted, you know. Clark and Alexander too. But somehow now I'm here, I prefer this. They'd be down in Caserta signing official documents of surrender in the Victor Emmanuel Palace and nobody would get to see them except the big brass. But this is a people's war, Sergeant. Though I'm not a Communist, that's what it is all right, and they should be in on the end of it just like today. Gosh, it's great. Boy, oh, boy, I can't wait to get home to tell everybody."

"You're Italian, aren't you?"

"What do you think? You betcha. New York. You too?"

"Albany."

"Your people from Sicily?"

"Naples. Yours?"

"Rome." He looked Sicilian to me, the dark skin, the nose, the squat body. "Now about this gold," he drew closer and started whispering. "Maybe we can stall them until the Fifth Army and General Crittenberger get here. They're due any hour. They could take charge of it."

"The colonel won't wait. He knows that. He's got to do something now. You'll have to make a decision. Either give it to him or take charge of it yourself. Don't you have the authority?"

"Maybe I do. But once you show them the hiding place, they could just grab the loot and run and the hell with my authority."

"Make a deal."

"What kind of deal?"

"Give him a share. Nobody knows how much there is in the cases. Give some to him personally."

"You mean buy him off?"

"Why not?"

"Isn't he a Communist?"

"He's human and he's an Italian." I smiled. "You've been in military government long enough to know that bribing and paying off are a way of life here. Everybody's corruptible except the Pope."

He grinned back at me. "You got an idea there, Sergeant. You interested in some of the gold too?"

"I'm not that human or that Italian." He laughed.

Gentile called that he was ready to go. We had delayed long enough. So we all got back into the imperial green Alfa Romeo with the ivory steering wheel and started for the Como road and the Fascist treasury. It was agreed as we drove along that the major would bring the cases back to his room at the Gallia and a couple of partisan guards would be posted outside the door. Then he and the colonel would go to the Palazzo Cusani to see General Cadorna, head of CLNAI, and make plans to hand everything over to Italian authorities when the Fifth Army arrived.

112

I was skeptical of the idea yet I kept quiet and let the two of them arrange the details. The main thing was to give the gold to the Allies or the new government of the country and come out of this war with a clean conscience and my life. I frankly couldn't see being killed by the very people I had supported and whose side I was on. Still, at the same time, something told me not to remember exactly where I had hidden the stuff, to delay these guys as long as I could, hoping a tank squadron would come along.

"Now where is the building you said you put the cases in?" the colonel turned around in his seat as we passed a line of apartment houses. Moving farther and farther from the center of the city and the crowds and the traffic and into a run-down neighborhood.

"Not yet. Remember it was dark. Every place looked the same to me. You know where we stopped, Giuseppe, Mario? The place where we last got benzina?"

"No, no," Giuseppe protested. Mario sat silent, stiff, gazing down at his feet.

We crawled by a series of warehouses and factories, some tenement houses, then open fields of brown grass and debris. We were moving out into the country. A sign facing the other way announced Milano, but I couldn't make out the kilometers.

"Around here I think. On the other side of the road. Better go slow."

We moved at the pace of someone walking, scrutinizing each area we passed. Suddenly there it was ahead, standing all by itself, abandoned, a small nondescript stone structure with boarded up windows and an open doorway. I hesitated to identify it, wanting to glide by and yet at the same time knowing I couldn't postpone the inevitable much longer.

"Okay, there, over there," I pointed. We stopped opposite the building and got out. The colonel told the driver to go and bring back a truck to carry all the treasure. The stubby guy nodded and spun around and raced toward the city. We walked across the road and

113

into the dusky area with its heavy urine smell. Newspapers and empty wine bottles littered the floor. A shabbier and grimmer place than I remembered from last night.

"Dovè il tesoro?" Gentile said in a deep hard voice as we poked around the interior. No more smiles.

"You sure, Sergeant, that this is the right spot?" the major said coming up to me. Then he whispered, "Stalling them?" There was a certain nervousness in his expression.

"Positive," I said out loud. "I'd know that smell anywhere." And I walked reluctantly over to a corner and yanked at a couple of boards. They came loose without much trouble, and everybody gathered around me. Down on my hands and knees, I pulled up the first black case. The contents jiggled around inside.

"Open it," the major said as I put it down and reached for the second one.

"You mean before I bring them all up?"

"Yeah, we want to see if it's the right stuff. If there really is something valuable in those things. Hell, they could be fakes." I gazed at him astounded, wondering what the hell he was thinking.

"Why not wait until we get back to the hotel?"

"No, no," Gentile commanded. And I looked around at the major, Giuseppe, Mario, the two partisan guards with guns drawn. They were all staring at the black cases.

"Okay, then." And I undid the straps and forced the lock. Up popped the top and there sprawling before us, lay a glittering array of every kind of jewel and stone imaginable—rings and necklaces and bracelets, silver and gold and diamonds. The colonel bent down and scooped up a handful of the expensive glitter and kissed it and then let the hard bright stuff sift through his fingers. The major too bent down and grabbed a fistful and did the same. The two guards and Mario and Giuseppe followed. I stood back in the half-light stunned by the wealth and the rapt expression on everybody's face. It was like breaking into an Egyptian tomb and discovering a fantastic treasure that had lain in the dust and twilight for centuries, sacred, inviolate, deadly.

"Quanti?" Gentile said.

"Five."

"Buono, buono." And everybody began helping me haul out the heavy cases one by one. When they were opened, the display of wealth looked even more dazzling against the rough floorboards and the cold crepuscular interior, currency as well as jewelry and gold. And I wondered how all this could possibly be guarded in a hotel room. Once the news got out the major's suite would be stormed, everybody in Milan demanding a piece of the treasury and claiming it belonged to the people. Wives wanting back the gold wedding rings they sacrified for the Ethiopian War. Shopkeepers insisting they had been unjustly taxed by the Fascists. Partisans demanding reparations. And then there were the Communists. They wouldn't relinquish their rights over the horde very easily.

"Molti, molti, lire," Gentile said to the major. "Everybody happy, no?" He forced a slight smile.

"Sure is some pile. I'll turn it over to General Crittenberger when he gets here. I bet Clark will be surprised."

"Ah, fine, okay, si, buono, buono," the Colonel continued to display that strange half-smile that had something spooky about it. The two guards now stood at the door watching us taking inventory. They were rough, blunt-faced kids, big calloused hands, long hair, cocky mouths, cold eyes. Each one looked motley in an Eisenhower jacket, British trousers, American combat boots, Italian army forage caps with Red stars on them, blue neckerchiefs.

I started to go outside. They stopped me, raising their Sten guns.

"Take a piss, that's all." I unbuttoned my fly to show what I wanted to do and smiled. They were adamant. I called to the colonel. He said something sharp and they let me pass. Hurrying around to the rear, I surveyed the land. Straight back about a hundred yards stood a cluster of trees. After glancing over my shoulder, I took off for it. Nobody followed or noticed. And when I slid into the shade, I plopped down in the long grass and waited. A good view of the building and the road. Nobody in sight yet and no traffic from either direction.

After about ten minutes a truck and the green Alfa Romeo approached from Milano and stopped. A couple of men got out of each vehicle, everybody carrying a machine gun. They disappeared and everything became quiet. I listened for a shot or a scream or a motor. Nothing. The blue sky, the breeze, the deep silence that descends on Sunday and reverberates.

I stood up to go and see what was happening when four muffled shots rang out and the two partisan guards appeared behind the building. One of them called my name over and over. But for some reason they didn't move across the field toward the trees. Instead they returned to the front again. And in no time the two vehicles took off for the city, both crowded. But it was hard to determine if the major, Mario, and Giuseppe were in them.

One hour passed and then two. I was sure they were coming back, or someone was waiting for me to return. But when nothing happened I decided to find out if there had been executions, certain in my mind now that the three of them had been killed in typical partisan fashion—lined up against a wall inside and mowed down.

It was mid-afternoon. A few cars sped by. People in Sunday clothes were out walking. They acted so casual compared to those in the center of the city as if this were no special day. Cautiously, I tiptoed to the back of the building, paused a moment, then moved around to the side and toward the front. Stopping, I bent down and picked up a stone, hesitated, threw it toward the road. The two kids who had acted as guards popped out of the doorway, Sten guns ready. As one dashed around the corner, I tripped him up. The gun flew from his hand, and I snatched it out of the dirt and got the drop on the two of them. They stood paralyzed, silent, staring, breathing hard. I was tempted to fire into their guts and watch them double up and drop as suddenly, and for some unaccountable reason, the urge to kill overwhelmed me. Checking the impulse, I ordered them to strip and head for the trees. At first they didn't understand. I demonstrated, and they peeled off everything in a hurry and sprinted in naked terror across the field like plucked chickens fleeing with a furious flutter. I fired round after round over their heads, releasing the pressure that had been building up inside.

No shells around, no blood, no evidence of any shooting. The same greasy old newspaper, the same urine smell. The boards were back in place. Not a sign anybody had been here for days.

Had it been a trick to make me think they shot the major and Giuseppe and Mario? I come running and they nail me? Then when that failed did they leave those kids to finish me off? One thing was clear, though, they had the gold now. And they weren't taking it to the Hotel Gallia.

I walked out to the road with a Sten gun slung from my shoulder and turned toward the city, holding a thumb up to every car that rattled by, tilting my cap with the Red star that I had taken from one of the guards, fingering the blue neckerchief. And I did resemble a partisan, I was convinced. I even felt like one in a way—weary, jaunty, and tough.

After about an hour of aimless walking a vehicle did stop, a blue Fiat. Coming from Milan, it shot past, braked hard, and then zoomed back, skidding to a halt. The door swung open and the driver thrust a Beretta out and ordered me to drop my Sten and get into the car.

Chapter 11

"This it?" I said, watching his eyes, a kind of brownish black. "I'm next after the major, Giuseppe, and Mario?"

"You kill Tony and Dominick?"

"I chased them away, that's all. Scared them. You left them to finish me off, didn't you? But you didn't trust them to do the job and came back. You were right. Who's next on your list? Captain Silvio at the Milano?"

"We no harm anyone, no major, Giuseppe, Mario. We shoot only those who are against us—Il Duce, Fascisti."

"And those who want to take the gold away from you."

"No, no, the gold belong to us." He stared hard at me, the long face lengthening and the dark eyes narrowing.

"What were those shots I heard? Firecrackers?"

"We no shoot the major, Giuseppe, Mario. You are wrong, Signor."

"We'll see if they turn up. Maybe you and the CLNAI control Milan right now. But it won't be long before the Fifth Army moves in. You know the Fifth Army?"

"Si, I know. I am not afraid of Americani."

"You ought to be. Because here they come." I glanced up into the rearview mirror. He did, too, at that instant. And the second he took his eyes off me, I snatched the gun away with a quick move, jamming the muzzle into his gut as hard as I could. He gasped, grimaced, and slumped down, searching into my face with those gritty little dark eyes.

"Now you shoot me, no?"

"Not right away. First you're going to tell me what you did with Americano major and amici and where your men took the gold."

"We take to Milano, let go, Signor." He hesitated. I screwed the gun deeper into his stomach.

"And the gold?"

"Palazzo Cusani."

"You mean the headquarters of the CLNAI?"

"Si. I do not think American army go there. Partigiani guard it bene. You start new war. No good, Signor. You no fight Italiani."

"No, not Italiani. But Communisti. Now out."

He opened the door and slid off the seat and stood on the road as I slipped behind the wheel and took off for the city, leaving him gazing after me, a straight tall, woodenlike figure.

The American flag was still flying outside Silvio's room at the Milano. I parked a block away and went in the back door of the hotel. No guard this time. Everything had calmed down since the morning—small crowds, little traffic, sporadic shooting. Even a tram was running. And the place was practically empty.

As I entered the room without knocking, Silvio and Barbatti were talking to a short, thin, middle-aged Italian who reminded me of an SI agent—the sharp face, tieless white shirt, dark pants, grayish stubble, smoking a cigarette.

"Where's the gold?" Silvo said and then introduced me to Scala.

"The partisans, or I should say, the Communists got it. Major Rosselli and my men are dead, I think. Shot. I escaped. They're after me. You too. They want to take care of us before the Fifth Army arrives. Colonel Gentile's the head of the assassination squad. They apparently don't want any word of the Dongo gold leaking

119

out. He claims it's over at CLNAI headquarters, all half billion. But it could be that the Commies have taken it out of the city where nobody will ever find it. Looks like the new Italy is going to start off looking worse than the old."

"Christ, what a mess!"

"Going to see General Cadorna about it?"

"He'll deny any knowledge of it or the murders."

"I say, then, we get the hell out of here fast and go hunting for the Fifth Army. It's the only way we're going to survive now, Captain. We're marked, the only Americans in the city."

"Suppose we can't find them. They've been delayed or something."

"Then we better find a good hiding place. What about Colonel Rauff over at the Regina you were worrying about?"

"He's secure. Don't worry. They won't get him. You kill Gentile?"

"You kidding? I just left him stranded. He'll turn up pretty soon."

There was silence. Then Silvio thought of sending Scala to scout around and see what was happening, find out who might be coming after us and when, discover where the Fascist treasury was and how many were guarding it.

"If we can locate it. That's right, Sergeant. We don't have any other choice. We've got to show these guys they can't go around being the government and taking the law into their own hands, killing Americans, knocking off whoever they feel like, stealing gold. We've got to stop the bastards. And the best way to do that is to hit them where it hurts and where they least expect it."

Scala didn't need the instructions translated. He leaped out of the room in a flash. And while we waited for him to return, we swapped stories of the horror show in the Piazzale Loreto this morning. Silvio described how someone put Il Duce's head on his mistress's lap and then placed a mock scepter in his hand.

120

And to take pictures photographers propped up the celebrated chin with a rifle butt. When Claretta was first strung up, her skirt fell over her head revealing her naked thighs, and the women screamed in protest until someone tied the skirt between her legs. Barbatti relished telling how he saw a big guy in shirtsleeves, his hairy arms caked with blood, pick up one Fascist body after another and lift it high in the air as if he were auctioning off the poor stiff. People were cheering and laughing, cursing and yelling. At one point they became so unruly that the partisans had to fire over their heads and bring out hoses to prevent a stampede.

And as we talked the whole scene came back to me along with the memory of Il Duce before the war. And I wondered if I would ever get over the contrast. Some terrible fury had been let loose in the world all right. I could feel it in my bones. Like this afternoon at that stone hut, wanting in the worst way to pull the trigger and blast those two kids I didn't know from Adam. Christ, when would it end? And where?

Twilight and still no sign of Scala. We had a couple of salami sandwiches and some coffee, and then the talk turned to the States and OSS in Italy and the war in the Far East. How many of us would go on to China and fight with the Communists in Yenan? Once I thought it would be great, but now I confessed that I had had enough of guerrilla warfare for one lifetime. Silvio and Barbatti said they wouldn't mind heading out there and taking on the Japs. This wasn't a bad way to spend the war. Yeah, but I reminded them they had been in Berne for most of it working with Dulles, not sweating out some mission behind the lines. They changed the subject to what they were going to do first when they got home.

About five-thirty Scala returned. He looked tired, dispirited. Speaking rapidly in Italian, he said that he heard the Fascist tesoro was now at the Prefecture on Corso Monforte, the same place where Mussolini and his convoy departed for Lake Como on Wednesday. The Communists evidently didn't think anybody would look there. And it wouldn't embarrass the CLNAI and General Cadorna. Besides, they could guard the courtyard easily and prevent anyone from breaking in and stealing the stuff.

Silvio asked him what was the best way to get into the place. He advised against any direct assault. It wouldn't work. Too many guards, too inaccessible. I had an idea. Why not use the furniture van we brought from Dongo? No one would suspect us. Scala could drive. I could hide in the back. The old Trojan horse trick. Ride in and locate the cases and carry them out. It shouldn't take more than fifteen minutes. But, then, Silvio wanted to know, where would we go from there? That was the question. Well, if we couldn't find a safe house in the city and the Fifth Army hadn't arrived by that time, maybe we could return to Dongo. He vetoed that plan. We had to keep the gold here. Why not bring it back to this hotel? No, that would jeopardize his mission, make more difficult the surrender of the Germans in Italy. OSS was working out with General Wolff. Did he want us to try to get back the treasury or not? Yes, he wanted that. We had to do it. But he still wasn't convinced my scheme was the best.

Scala liked my idea and thought it might have a chance despite the guards at the gate. Everybody by now knew about the yellow furniture van and associated it with the partisans and the execution of the Fascists. Nobody would suspect that I was inside. So as soon as it got dark, he and I started for the Piazzale Loreto where I was sure we would find the truck since I had seen it parked there that morning. And I still had the ignition key that Giuseppe had given me.

We drove to the square, and spotted the lorry standing by the curb and looking abandoned like the whole place, only the debris from the morning madness drifting across the stones. The skeleton gas station outlined against the sky with its cement beams and steel girders gave the whole area an eerie atmosphere. I could still see those bodies swaying in the breeze, hear the mob cheering and jeering. Occasionally a car shot through the open space from one of the five streets.

We stopped and gazed around and then got into the truck and tried to start the motor. Out of gas. Scala said he knew where there was some petrol, and he charged across the city after it in his car, stealing two cans off the rear of a disabled German lorry he located on a back street.

After we finished gassing up, we sat in the cab until midnight trying to figure out the best way to enter the Prefecture, Palazzo Monforte, a fortresslike building with a courtyard, a barracks in back, and an iron gate. I thought we could pull the body trick again. I lie under the canvas and make it appear as if Scala were transporting the bodies of Mussolini and his mistress back to the place where they had started their fatal flight to the Valtellina five days ago. No one would question that or take a good look since everybody had had enough, I believed, of the battered old dictator's body. And the guards would recognize the van. Of course, if anybody did get curious, I would take care of him quietly, lethally. I showed Scala a long-bladed knife I had picked up in Silvio's room.

He grinned at the plan and talked of the gold as if it were a woman he was going to lay. A member of the Action Party, he said that he hated the Communists and would do anything to frustrate them. The idea of my posing as the dead Mussolini he enjoyed too, and wished we had a pair of jackboots to stick out from under the canvas to make the sight more authentic in case a guard did look inside the van.

How he talked his way into the courtyard of the Prefecture I don't know. But we were inside in no time, parked and alone. A few lights in the surrounding windows but mainly the place was dark, deserted. After climbing the spiral staircase, we paused on the first floor and looked for the office where he said the cases were supposed to be. A guard, stocky and dressed in partisan style, Red star and tricolored neckerchief, stood outside

123

the door, machine gun in hand. Scala put a finger to his mouth and I got my Sten ready. He motioned for my knife and then slipped away from me without a sound, the weapon inside his jacket.

I watched him. He walked slowly, casually toward the man, who began to laugh at the little guy. Maybe it was something he said or some expression on his face. There was a Charlie Chaplin aura about him, his walk, his gestures. Closer and closer. And the guard didn't challenge him. His gun hung loose at his side. Suddenly he was on the floor without a sound, curled up like a fetus, clutching himself, out cold. Not a drop of blood. Scala waved, and I tiptoed toward him.

"Dead?" I whispered. He put a finger to his mouth and smiled, gave the body a slight kick. It moved.

He took a step forward and soundlessly opened the door. A large dusky room dimly lit. A thick carpet with the Fascist emblem embroidered on it. Fancy gilt-trimmed mahogany furniture. Romulus and Remus painted on the ceiling. But no cases anywhere. Instead four men stood in the center with machine guns. At first I thought of firing my weapon and letting happen what may. But I froze. Scala grinned in that sly, faint way of his. One of the four was Gentile.

"You come for the gold, Americano," he smirked. "Where is your capitano?"

"With the Fifth Army."

"They come here?"

"On their way."

"To help you?"

"We thought—"

"Ah, si, we know what you think. You drop the gun. We talk about the gold, no? You like to see cases you bring to Milano?" He continued to grin at me.

I gazed around, listened, not quite certain what to do, thinking if I drop the gun he will definitely shoot the daylights out of me. And if I fire he will definitely kill me.

"Signor, drop your gun. Subito." His voice had the

124

familiar military ring, deep and harsh and implacable.

"How did you know we were coming?"

He didn't answer. I looked away into a dim corner as if catching sight of something alarming. The moment their eyes turned with mine I squeezed the trigger and let go with a burst right at the armed men. Then I ran like hell out of the room and down the hall and the marble steps nd into the courtyard to the van, bullets flying everywhere. I started the motor, my foot pushing the pedal to the floor, and took off, careening out of the Palazzo past the guards at the gate and through a furious fusillade drumming on the sides. Out into the empty black street, not knowing where to go. Driving crazily, feverishly, all the time wondering if Scala had set me up.

A single car sped after me and was gaining with each block. When I reached the Duomo and the piazza in front, the truck stalled and went dead. I jumped out and started running for my life. The car behind zoomed after me. No one shooting yet. Bearing down faster and faster, the motor thundering in my ears. Headlights making me a big bright target. I had a premonition this was it. I would never reach the building ahead safely before the damn thing struck, and I strained with all my might to get as close to the wall as I could. The engine kept growing louder and louder. The lights grew sharper and sharper. Still no gun fired. And that seemed strange unless whoever was at the wheel was intent on a hit and run.

Just when I felt the vehicle was about to smash into me, the noise, deafening now, the smell of heat and gasoline overwhelming, I dropped to the pavement and rolled to the right. The driver kept on coming. He couldn't swerve or stop quick enough, and with a scream of brakes and a squealing of skidding tires he smacked into the building.

For a moment I lay there on the stones not thirty feet away from the wreck, listening to the explosion, watching the flames shoot up, feeling the searing heat. I couldn't believe that I was still alive, my neck stiff, sore all over, blood trickling down my legs.

Jumping up, I raced toward Piazza della Scala, searching for Via Manzoni before somebody else arrived. It couldn't be far to the Milano. And I kept on going, though pretty much out of breath, weakening fast, wondering if I would make it. A car approached. Huge headlights picked me up. I darted into a doorway. A machine gun shattered the quiet of the street and the noise echoed. The car roared off and then spun around and slammed back. But before it reached me I sprinted across to the hotel and for the first time in days spotted American uniforms, heard familiar voices. It was like coming home after an all-night party, drunk and disoriented, only vaguely remembering anything or anyone.

"Hey, this hotel has been taken over by Americans," a major staggered up to me. He was drunk.

"I'm an American," I said, barely able to talk, feeling myself buckling at the knees.

"An American?" he gaped in my face. "What the hell are you doing in that Eyetie suit?"

"I'm with OSS. Behind the lines. I've got to see Captain Silvio, head of the mission here. He in his room?"

"Never heard of him. What's this OSS crap?"

"Intelligence organization. He's supposed to be in 407." And I groped my way toward the lift before the tall, lean, Texas-sounding officer started getting too curious.

"Hey, you guys," he cried out to a group of officers in the lobby, "there goes one of our secret agents." The door closed and the cab shot up.

I walked into the room and there stood Lieutenant Barbatti in khaki shorts, undershirt, stocking feet, a drink in one hand.

"What the hell's going on, Del Greco?"

I brushed past him and collapsed on the chair.

"Where's the captain?"

126

"Out."

"With a woman?"

"Jesus, no. You crazy? Over at the Palazzo Cusani to see General Cadorna and the CLNAI committee. He's trying to establish formal communications with the partisans. Clark's pissed off about the bloody circus at the Piazzale Loreto this morning. He says either the nonsense stops or he'll declare martial law in the city and confiscate every weapon. The partisans are supposed to hand in theirs anyway. The war's over. We don't want any Red government up here."

"For the Commies it's not over, not by a long shot. It's just beginning. They fixed Scala tonight. And they nearly got me. It's a miracle I'm alive. I don't know how it happened."

"You find the Fascist treasury?"

"They set us up. Or maybe Scala did. I don't know. But the whole thing was a trap from the beginning. I gotta get out of this town, Lieutenant. Ten to one the captain never comes back from that meeting with the CLNAI."

"They wouldn't harm him. They wouldn't dare. Clark would order the city searched, General Cadorna imprisoned along with all the partisan leaders of the CLNAI, the Communist Party banned."

"I don't know. They've got to eliminate everybody who knows anything about the Fascist gold. The bastards have stolen it."

"I'll call over and see if he's still alive and kicking."

He went to the phone on the table, dialed the Palazzo and seemed to be talking to the captain, though I couldn't hear any voice on the other end. He would be back at the hotel in an hour or so. Negotiations were going on and he couldn't leave.

"You better hit the sack, Del Greco," he said after hanging up. He studied me as he sipped on his drink. "You've had a hard day." He went across the room and sat down.

"You can say that again. It's one I'll never forget."

"Me neither. Wasn't that some circus at Loreto? I suppose Mussolini was a stinking bastard, but, you know, I kind of felt sorry for him, hanging there like some dead animal and all those people giving him the raspberry."

"The captain talking to them about the gold?"

"He didn't say."

"He should." I paused and scrutinized him. Skinny-looking out of uniform with those small sly eyes you couldn't see into, he made me uneasy. "You didn't tell him I got back, did you?"

"He was too busy to go into that. You can tell him about you and Scala when he comes in. And don't worry, Del Greco, about anybody harming you. Crittenberger's here. You're safe. See all the GI's in the lobby?"

"I wonder if I'll ever be safe again. You and the captain ever hear about the gold in Switzerland?"

"Not a word. Dulles was too wrapped up in the surrender operation with Wolff. I don't think it's as important as you believe."

"Maybe not. I better go lie down."

"Yeah, you better, kid. You look bad."

And I staggered into the next room and plopped down on the bed. Only once did I wake up. Voices were talking in the other room, and someone was saying, "We gotta do something with him. He's too dangerous." But I couldn't tell who was speaking or what he was speaking about. It just sounded angry and ominous. And I wanted to get up and go over to the door and listen some more, peek out. But I didn't have the strength to move. Every muscle ached. And my throat was too dry to cry out or even utter a word. Then I passed out for good.

Chapter 12

When I woke up it was mid-morning. Everybody had left the suite. Traffic was humming down in the street. The American flag still flying from the balcony. I went out there, thinking of yesterday and the bodies swinging in the gas station, the crowd shouting and milling around, the major talking excitedly about seeing history made. All that gone now. A new day, a new week, a new world. Everything flowing normal and quiet once again as if there had been no bloody opera to end the war and maybe not even any war at all. Just another drunken weekend. I certainly felt as if I had a hangover.

The door opened and Scala stood on the threshold smiling.

"Christ, I thought you were dead!" I cried out as if seeing a ghost. He grinned.

"They take me prisoner. I escape. I find the gold."

"Oh, no, not that again. No more. I'm finished with the stuff. I'm getting the hell out of here in one piece. Fuck the gold, the Commies, Italy, the army, the whole show."

"Como," he gaped at me. "They take the gold to Cernobbio near Como. Villa Castlenuovo on the lake. We go, no?"

"Yeah, and get our balls shot off. Not unless the Fifth Army goes with us."

"Trento, quaranta chilometri. I have car. It is easy. Very fast. Few guards. Okay, what you say, Victor?"

"Sorry. Whoever told you that story was lying and

129

trying to set another trap for us. The cases are still in this city if they're anywhere, hidden under a big Red star."

"Dove?"

"Communist headquarters probably. Maybe even the Archbishop's palace in Piazza del Duomo where I heard that Mussolini had his meeting with the CLNAI before he left for Como."

"Possible." He kept staring at me.

"Okay, you win. One last try before calling it quits. We've come this far, I guess. But first we've got to find Captain Silvio. We're not going to get anywhere here without him." He grinned at me in that nervous, excited way of his.

We went into Via Manzoni searching for Silvio and Barbatti, first around La Scala and the Duomo and then up to the Piazza Della Republica and the Statione. Over to the Prefecture on Corso Monforte. Finally to CLNAI headquarters at Palazzo Cusani. And, Christ, if there weren't the two of them marching out of the building toward their Alfa Romeo. They spotted us and waited.

"Scala's got another line on the gold."

"Forget it, Del Greco, there's no such thing as the Dongo gold. It's a fake, a Fascist fake. I just talked to General Cadorna again and he says the whole story is a fabrication."

"But I saw it, captain. I had my hands on it. There were jewels and wedding rings and millions and millions of lire and lots of gold bullion. It was real. Why else was major Rosselli shot?"

"He wasn't. You were wrong about that. He's at the Gallia feeling fine. I just talked to him."

"What about the two partisans with me, Giuseppe and Mario?"

"I don't know. He didn't mention them. They probably took off. You know the way these partisans are, here today and gone tomorrow."

"So you're going to believe him and forget it?"

"That's right. And I want you to do the same. I don't want you going around spreading crazy rumors and

130

stirring up people unnecessarily. It'll just create a lot of ill will and confusion.''

"You threatening to silence me too?''

"I'm telling you for your own good, Sergeant. Lay off the phony gold story.''

"Then you must be in on it, you and the Lieutenant. They must have bought you off. The major too.''

"Why you dirty little son-of-a-bitch!'' He put a hand on the .45 holstered on his hip.

"You going to take care of me now,'' I glared back at him, "just like the Commies?''

"Look, you dumb bastard, I'm telling you the Fascist treasury was a fake. And I'm ordering you to quit hunting for it. If you don't you're going to make my job that much more difficult.''

"Next I suppose you're going to tell me the Commies don't exist either and they never shot Mussolini or executed his ministers in Dongo. And everything that's happened to me up there and to this country in the last couple of days is all a dream.''

"OSS has officially given up interest in locating any Fascist gold. That's that. You do the same.''

"And if I don't?''

"Then you'll suffer the consequences, wise guy. And I won't be responsible for what happens to you.''

He and the Lieutenant drove off in the jeep, and Scala and I stood watching them.

"What do you think?'' I asked.

"Finito,'' he said sadly, "finito.''

"You believe him? After what we went through a little while ago at the Prefecture. They didn't act last night as if there wasn't any gold. And you said you heard a rumor where it's supposed to be hidden.''

"Si, Victor, but OSS say no treasure. Possible capitano and Communisti make agreement. They give him molti, molti lire and he say no gold. What you think?''

"Yeah, maybe. Silvio could even be tied in with a Captain D'Alessandro in the Pontiac mission and both

131

of them connected with the Mafia. We've got some of them in OSS. We used them in Sicily. The only thing to do is to find General Crittenberger, I guess, and tell him what's up.''

The more I thought about it the more I began to see that maybe there was some kind of comprehensive conspiracy after all. First, the major's death to prevent him from coming to Como and seizing Mussolini and the gold. Then Silvio denying its existence and making sure Giuseppe and Mario vanish. Now the attempt to put me out of action permanently. Hell, maybe there could even have been a deal whereby Silvio coming from Switzerland last week purposefully misses Mussolini and lets the Commies shoot him instead of taking him prisoner and transporting him to Caserta. They get the bodies for propaganda and the bulk of the gold and he and his Mafia friends the lire and their link to the new power in Italy. But if all that was the case, nobody was going to let me contact the army very soon to tell my story. There was no point in going back to the hotel and talk to any officer. Silvio would spot me.

So we drove around the city, and near the Galleria sighted a couple of lieutenants with yellow, blue, and red triangular First Armored Division shoulder patches. I told Scala to stop and leaped out after them. One was stocky with streaks of gray in his hair, the other tall and thin and youthful-looking with black hair. They wore Eisenhower jackets and carried .45's on their belts. Civilians were coming up to shake their hands and kiss them, offer flowers, smiling.

At first they thought I was an Italian, and it took my dog tags and some GI lingo to convince them I was genuine U.S. Army, although they protested that they had never heard of OSS and couldn't help me. I'd have to go to headquarters, and they didn't know where that was at the moment. Maybe at Osnago. Everything was fluid, units spreading out in every direction and blocking the main routes into the city. They had just arrived.

"Where's your outfit?" the hefty one sized me up,

maybe thinking I was AWOL.

"It's not. I'm the only one left. Everybody's been wiped out. I was the radio operator for a behind-the-lines mission over at Lake Orta. I've got to have protection and fast."

"Why?"

"I know too damn much about what's happened to the Fascist gold."

"Fascist gold?" the thin one said. "What the hell's that?"

"It's why Mussolini was killed. He was carrying half a billion dollars worth of stuff. I know who stole it and they know I know and are out looking for me. I've got to find General Crittenberger."

"You've had too much vino, kid?" the stocky officer said. "Come on, Dan, let's get soused and find a couple of Eyetie women with plenty of this grazie stuff."

He and the other lieutenant drifted off into the Galleria. I wanted to run after them and yell, "Where the hell are you going? You can't leave me." But they obviously couldn't care less.

"What do we do now?" Scala said.

"Go to Firenze, I guess, where the OSS Detachment is and tell our story. That's all we can do."

"Communisti shoot us. They find us."

"Maybe. But we sure as hell can't stay here. We're easy targets."

Scala was skeptical about leaving the area. He still insisted that we ought to go to Como to search for the gold. The man who had told him about it, Geno Terzi, said a Communist named Luigi Ferrari was in charge. He had been in the Fifty-second Garibaldi Brigade and was a good friend of Togliatti, Longo, and Lampredi. It had been taken out of Milano so that the Americans wouldn't capture it. That's what they were afraid of now, Americani and Inglesi coming and destroying their plans both for the gold and seizing Nord Italia."

"He wasn't lying to you? Setting up another trap?"

"No, no lie, no trap. I know him. Buono. I trust him.

We fight Tedeschi Bolazno, Cortina. You believe me, Victor?"

"Maybe."

"He say they use gold to start Communist state in Italia. Like Russia. Non buono. We have new war."

"Okay, let's try it. Anything's better than staying around here now I guess. I don't imagine anybody in the Fifth Army will believe our story until we have some proof to back it up. Still—"

"You think I fool you, Victor? I no Communista. At Prefecture you run, I am prisoner. Then I jump out of window and they find me. But I escape. Amico, Victor, buono, buono amico." He looked at me appealingly.

We hit Corso Garibaldi and the road to Como and set out for the lake country. It was noon. People crowding the streets going about their normal business. Tram cars and bicycles swelling the traffic. Although I still had my doubts about Scala and wondered if I shouldn't go south on my own, his story made sense and he acted sincere. After all he was one of our agents. Or at least Silvio indicated that he was. Besides, I told myself, there must be GI's around Lake Como I could contact if I got in trouble. Obviously, the captain had disassociated himself from me here and possibly even hoped that I would be eliminated by the Commies.

We stopped at a cafe to grab a sandwich and a cup of coffee and relax. When we started up, a vehicle was trailing us at a discreet distance, a brown Fiat 1100 with two men in front. I kept one eye on the rearview mirror.

"I don't think we're going to make Como," I said. "Look behind you."

He turned around and then smiled at me. "Niente, niente. They do not shoot us. They think we lead them to tesoro."

"You know them?"

"Si, Dante Volpicelli and Leo Valiani. Action Party. Work for Parri."

"They know where we're headed?"

"They know we after tesoro. Soon, Victor, everybody be after l'oro, no? Fifth Army, Eighth Army, Italian Army, Carabinieri, Communisti, Socialisti. All Italia."

"Jesus, you mean we're joining a damn gold rush?"

"Ah, si, gold rush like in your country. Make everybody rich, no?"

It didn't make sense somehow, and yet the longer we sped on and the farther back the Fiat stayed, the clearer it was becoming that maybe he was right.

"Hey, you know what? I bet we're taking the same route Mussolini did six days ago."

"Is that bad, Victor? You afraid apparizioni?"

"No, I'm not superstitious. It's just that I've been following that guy around so long and seeing so many people killed because of him I'm nervous. Maybe even clairvoyant."

"We not go to Como?"

"Maybe we should find an American unit and tell them where the gold is and then head south to Firenze."

"Possible they no find gold and they say you take it. You help Communisti, Mafiosi. Capisce?"

I was slowly beginning to. Too deep into the whole affair now to pull out and forget everything that had happened. Too many people dead, too much money at stake, too large a crisis for postwar Italy hanging in the balance. So it was on to Como. And who knows after that what lay ahead—Cernobbio, Meaggio, Musso, Dongo. Hell, everything could end up in that little town square with a firing squad at my back and the lake and the Valtellina in front of me. Not a happy prospect. But as we drove on and talked of other things—of home and girls and the future—life didn't seem too bad at the moment. Confusing, turbulent, hopeless. But that was Italy for you. People standing around primitive and poor and shabby. But not tragic. No matter how grim the situation nothing stayed that way long in this volatile country. Only the chaos and the uncertainty endured, and you learned to live with them.

Chapter 13

Although Como was full of GI's, they didn't look any more friendly than the blue neckerchiefs on our tail, who despite Scala's identification I still thought might be Communists. So we drove around town trying to lose them, past the Statione and out to the Stadio and along Lungo Lario from where you could see the lake and villas and great terraced gardens. Then to Via Borgovico and the road north. I hoped whoever was following would think we were headed for Lugano 33 kilometers away. And outside of town we did lose them, or maybe they just gave up.

We pulled into Villa Castlenuovo just beyond Cernobbio about four o'clock. It looked deserted. An avenue of cypress, a great white mansion with a park and tropical garden and across the lake mountain peaks. Twilight spreading out over the cold gray water like a fine mist.

"A trap?" I asked Scala. He stopped the car inside the high grilled gate.

"No, no, il tesoro is here. I know, I know."

"You mean they would leave it unguarded? You're crazy. Either it's a trap or somebody tricked you. Nobody's around. Look, even the windows are boarded."

We got out and tramped the paths, guns drawn. Flowers and bushes and hedges were everywhere, filling the air with a heavy fragrance. Classical statuary loomed through the dusk. If anyone wanted to hide the gold here, it seemed like the ideal spot—isolated, only a narrow road in through the trees, the lake out there easily watched. The only sound the lap of water and the gentle sweep of the wind.

"Who in the hell told you about this place?"

"I tell you, Geno Terzi. He say partigiani take Fascist tesoro from Milano Sunday night."

"Yeah, but why here?"

"Safe. No Americani, no Inglesi. I believe him. He sincero."

"Well, he gave you a bum steer this time. There's nobody. Not even a sign anyone's been here since the war began. What I can't figure out, though, is why would he want to mislead you, especially if it's not a trap."

"Maybe rumor he hear."

"You give him lire?"

"Si, molti lire. Bad?"

"Very bad."

"Go to Dongo?"

"Oh, no, not there again." I studied him and the town came back to me in all its shabby gloom, the high dark hills and the shallow bay with the shadows floating across the water. "Why go there? That doesn't make sense."

"Why we come here? Il oro."

"The Commies wouldn't bring it back there."

"No one suspect. I hear other rumor. They say you bring only part of Fascist tesoro to Milano. There is molti, molti lire you not take."

I stared at him for a couple of minutes and said nothing, stunned. Then, Christ, it dawned on me! My God, maybe he was right! Why not? Bruna and her brother could have shown D'Alessandro only part of the wealth the Fascists were carrying in that convoy and maybe not the biggest part at that. The rest could be secretly guarded somewhere in town. And maybe Father

Bernado would know where. He did act strange, come to think of it, scared too and close-mouthed. He could be the one to unlock the mystery of the whole thing, put his finger on those behind the operation.

"Okay, we go to Dongo," I said, feeling the gold fever stirring in me once more as well as the old urge to get this damn thing over once and for all and end at least my part in the war.

Dusk was deepening as we drove up the winding narrow road through the string of little towns that I remembered so vividly from last week. No barricades now, no stopping and showing passes. The celebrations had ended. Candles in the windows, families sitting down to supper. On one side the water darkening and on the other hills thrusting up in huge black masses. An overhanging quiet in the air. Tunnels and bridges and sharp curves. Steep rock face. A horse-drawn wagon crawling along with a lantern swinging between the rear wheels. A biting wind blowing off the lake.

Although it was hard to believe a priest would be working with the Communists to steal gold, he certainly seemed to be a good friend of Bruna and her brother. Obviously it was through them that the captain found the hiding place for the cases. And he could know through them too if there was more loot hidden in town. Possibly he was hiding it himself and that was the reason for his nervousness when we were there. It could be the reason, too, why he let me take the cases without much protest, hoping it would get rid of D'Alessandro. But then I thought of another angle. Suppose the captain did know he had only part of the treasury. He had worked out a deal with the Commies. After all he was supposed to have ties with Togliatti and Longo, old Spanish Civil War buddies. But then why would he worry about sneaking the loot out of town unless he felt he had the whole treasury and not just the promised part and was doublecrossing his old pals? Weird. Complicated. The more I thought about it the more incredible it all became.

As we rode through the night, my mind drifted away . from the questions and the mystery and concentrated on the route we were taking, the same one Il Duce had followed last Thursday and Friday. And I started speculating again on the doomed old man and what he must have been thinking of while traveling his last mile. Not about how much was in his government's treasury, that was a cinch. About Claretta maybe and her thick black hair and big warm breasts and long sexy legs, his wife back in Cernobbio, Hitler at Munich and the Brenner Pass in the good old days when the two of them were always meeting, the balcony of the Palazzo Venezia with thousands below cheering and shouting his name. Or about his son-in-law, Count Ciano, whom he had executed. And I wondered what goes through the mind of somebody about to die who has himself sent so many to their deaths.

We stopped to eat in Musso, and I told Scala about what had happened in Dongo and why I thought Father Bernado could help us if we could get him to talk. Then after looking at an old ruined Medici fortress, we headed up the hill past remnants of the partisan blockade at Vall'Orba. It was almost eight o'clock.

"If anyone recognizes me," I said, "it could be bad for both of us. They might mistake me for one of the firing squad and run me out of town. Most of the people were against those executions."

"Victor, non parla Italiano. I find Father Bernado and ask him questions. He tell me the truth. If not, I say the devil come and get him." He laughed.

"You're not going to talk to anybody else?"

"Nobody. Solo il padre. Nobody see me, nobody know."

It was a steep climb and then a quick drop down into Dongo and the square facing the bay. Empty now. The town appeared deserted. We stopped and looked around and the whole grim scene of last Saturday came back to me, fifteen doomed men ripped by bullet after bullet. No sign of that terrible evening hour remained. Just the lake, the jetty, the low wall, the War Memorial, the public urinal. Across the way the town hall stood dimly lit. The silence was like that of a cemetery except for the lap of the water.

The church wasn't far off, and in no time we were parked outside the rectory. Waiting a few minutes before climbing out, we listened, checked the area. We hadn't seen anybody yet and only a few isolated lights. Either most of the people had left, superstitious about the executions, or they had locked themselves in their houses afraid to go out. A spooky place all right, shadowy, silent, almost sinister.

"I see him, Victor. I talk to padre. You stay. I come back quick if it is safe."

"How long will you be?"

"A few minutes. If I not come back quick, you go to mountains. No come in to see me. Capisce? Okay?"

"Be careful."

"I not like. I see no one in church. No light. Strano, molto strano. What do you think?"

"Yeah, very strange. Keep your gun handy."

"In Italia always people are in church. Here nothing. Non buono."

"A regular ghost town all right," I said, thinking of the places we had passed through driving up the lake. Although they were quiet, at least there were signs of life.

"Si, si, ghost town. I am worried."

"Want me to go in with you? I met Father Bernado. He'll recognize me. I was only here a couple of days ago."

"No, no," he said flatly. "I go, Victor. You stay. Much better. You guard automobile. I talk to padre."

He disappeared into the dark stone buildings. I got out of the car and studied the street again. Still no sound of a motor or a voice or a footstep anywhere. No gunfire in the distance. No lights. One, two, three minutes ticked away. Suddenly Scala burst out of the rectory and ran up to me. He was out of breath, shaking, not able to speak. Finally he whispered, "Vieni, vieni, Victor. Pronto, pronto. Very bad."

He raced back into the parish house and along a dim hallway and through a series of low-ceilinged rooms until he reached a small one lit with a bare bulb and containing a desk, a crucifix, holy pictures, statues, and on the stone floor staring up at us the blood-soaked body of the black-clothed priest. It was Father Bernado —the tall frame, the thin drawn face, the skull-like head, lips tight in death as in life. Shot at close range in the stomach.

"Communisti?"

"Possible," Scala said, staring down at the corpse.

"Or the American capitano I told you about. He could have come back here if he heard I hadn't taken all the cases. I thought I got him with a grenade on the road to Milan. But it could have been someone else."

"Terribile, terribile, Victor! Kill padre."

"Christ, if it was the captain, I don't know! I'll finish him for good this time. So help me God! First the major and now this."

"Possibile in Dongo. Not dead long." He felt the body. "They know we come. They fear he tell you about gold, no?"

"They ought to rename this town Dis, the city in hell. We better get out of here before someone shows up and accuses us of the murder. We'd be lynched in the square." He looked at me puzzled. "Hung up like Il Duce in Piazzale Loreto."

"Where do we go?"

"Let's try Lake Orta. If the captain is behind this business, he wouldn't stay around here. And the only place he knows is Orta. He's got friends over there. It's close to Genoa. He was planning to smuggle out the gold from there."

141

"How about Communisti?"

"Maybe he made a deal with them. Who knows? He could be connected with some other people in OSS too. Even Captain Silvio in Milan. Didn't he tell us there wasn't any gold, we were crazy, the whole story was a fake? Christ, you can't trust anybody anymore."

"What if he is not there?"

"Well, at least we'll be safe. Nobody will be looking for us on that lake, I guarantee you that. No fighting over there and few Tedeschi. It won't be hard to find our way down to Firenze either. Not so much military traffic. What do you say? Okay?"

"Si, Victor, we go. I trust you." He smiled at me, and I felt here was one guy I could rely on, not greedy, political and conniving.

We rushed out to the car, leaving the priest lying on the stone floor. I thought about trying to find a housekeeper or another priest or someone who could take care of the corpse. But that would expose us, and there wasn't time to spend on the dead now.

The Fiat was gone. Not a sign of it anywhere. We looked at each other stunned. I started to say something when I heard voices coming down the street. We ran back into the rectory and out a side door into an alley beside the church. A shadowy figure stood at the end. Scala took out his Beretta. I walked toward the man alone, hands in the air, crying, "Resa, resa!" Making a noise with my feet to disguise Scala sneaking behind me along the shadowy wall on my right. Just as I reached the hefty figure in the leather jacket and military cap and started to talk to him, he came toward me holding a pistol. He started to speak. I waited. Scala jumped him from the side, and the big guy dropped to the ground. We dashed out of the confined space into the cobblestone street. No one around. All dark.

"How we go to Lake Orta?" he said, the Beretta still in his hand.

"Find a car. I'll go to the piazza and wait. You look

around for one. Then come there and signal with your lights twice. Capeesh?''

"Impossible."

"No, it's not. You've got to do it. How else are we going to get the hell out of here? I'd go with you, but I don't speak Italian too hot and somebody might recognize me from Saturday. Okay?''

"They know we are here, Victor. Bad, very bad."

"You're damn right it's bad. Could be the captain. Could be somebody he left behind. Maybe the Commies. They catch us and say we killed the poor guy. We hang for their murder. Capeesh?"

He nodded and shot out through the labyrinth of streets and unlighted buildings. I started in the direction of the square, mindful of the shadows and darting from doorway to doorway. Wondering all the time if the captain had returned and if the Pontiac mission had been planned with the Fascist treasury in mind and not with any phony liaison with the CLNAI. He could be working independent of SI and Corvo, even independent of OSS and the general. Coming over here to rob a whole damn country. Fantastic. But, Christ, OSS was a fantastic outfit with all kinds of unpredictable people from bankers to murder-for-hire experts. Who knows what the hell many of them were doing in the organization?

I reached the town hall and stood against the building waiting. All the time concentrating on the spot where the fifteen had been executed Saturday at sundown and recalling the scene: shots coming from a high window and the firing squad turning and raking the house and people screaming, then a hush settling over the square deeper and deeper followed by the staccato drilling of machine guns tearing into the bound bodies.

A car thundered into the piazza and stopped short, brakes squealing, headlights on, motor running. I waited. The lights blinked twice, Starting to spring across the vacant space, I hesitated for some inexplicable reason. Maybe it was the ghostly presence of the dead Fascists and the execution squad still haunting me and the superstitious fear of crossing the stones where they once stood. Or maybe the foreboding of the whole melancholy vista from the blind-looking buildings and the tenebrous lake to the stark mountains across the way. Or maybe just the fact that I hadn't heard anybody yet or seen any sign of life and suddenly there was the car and the signal.

The lights flicked off and on twice more. It felt strange for some reason. Something wrong. I picked up a small stone at my foot, waited, and hurled it as hard as I could toward the car. The metal rang out in the middle of that hollow stillness with a pinging sound and echoed. A spotlight flooded the area and without any warning guns from everywhere opened up. The green Fiat burst into flames and exploded, a tremendous pink and purplish glow shooting up into the night sky and hovering out over the water before falling and fading.

I ran behind the town hall and down a street, sticking close to the houses. Feet scuffling all around me. Shouting. More shots. I thought momentarily of Scala in that car and then rushed on searching for somewhere to hide—a doorway, an alley, a truck, a cart, anywhere to get away from the guns and the flames and the footsteps. The air reverberated with the explosion. The sky lit up. And I could feel myself shuddering from the impact of the fusillade and the boom when the gas tank erupted.

Windows lit up along the street. People dashed out of buildings hollering that the Tedeschi were bombing the town. Excited groups congregated, ignoring me as I slipped past them into the obscurity. Although I didn't know where the hell I was headed, I knew that I had to get as far away from the square as I could and had a dim idea of searching for the road to Germassio.

A hand caught my shoulder from behind, a hard firm hand. And just as I turned to hit the guy, I thought I recognized one of the men from the Fifty-second Garibaldi Brigade who had taken Il Duce and his mistress from Germasio to Mezzegra last Friday night and whom I had seen arguing with Colonel Valerio about shooting the Fascists in the square. A tall mustached man with narrow shoulders, wearing an Alpine hat topped by a feather but no Red star or tricolored neckerchief or armband.

"Who are you, Signor?" he asked in English.

"I am an American sergeant, Victor Del Greco. Who are you?"

"Giulio Pastore."

"I came here looking for an American captain who I think took the Fascist treasury. And I almost got blown up in the piazza. My friend was killed. He was Italiano."

"Ah, si, capisco."

"You know where the tesoro is? Who took it? Who killed my friend? I'm OSS. I was on a mission on Lake Orta, Second Garibaldi Division. Signor Moscatelli. We were supposed to go to Milano and capture Il Duce, send him to Caserta."

"You not do it, no?"

"That's right. Can you hide me? I don't know who is after me. Maybe the Reds. Maybe some Americani Mafiosi. Maybe both. Very bad."

"Signor, you come." I trotted behind him down a couple of steep passageways and under arches and behind some dark buildings and across empty streets. It was like walking in a catacomb. The sound of voices and guns diminished. In the country now. We approached a gate and walked into tree-covered grounds, a villa at the end of the road.

"Your home?"

"Si."

We entered a dusky hallway with carpeted stairs, and I peered into a high-ceilinged living room with a fireplace and a coat of arms over it, an Oriental rug, heavy dark antiques. The lights were low.

"No one come, Signor. You are safe here."

"I'm not so sure. Do you know what's going on?"

"Si," he said. "I know." He smiled. "Americani take gold and go away."

"Captain D'Alessandro?"

"I hear the name. He want gold, you want gold, partisans want gold, people of Dongo want gold." He looked at me with that big broad warm face, and I felt at ease.

"But I had a lot of it, you see. Five cases, in fact. They were in the church near the piazza. The captain put them there and was planning on smuggling them out of the country. He thought he had the whole Fascist treasury. And I got them away from him and brought everything to Milan to give to the Allies. Then the Communists stole them from me. But the Italiano killed in the square, an agent working for OSS, he said he heard that I only took part of the tesoro. There was more hidden in Dongo. You follow me?"

"Capisco. Partisans take molti, molti lire to Como. Luigi Renaldi come and put cases in Fiat and go. He give Americani gold and lire too. Then they go. I not know where."

"I bet I do. Lake Orta. How about helping me track them down? They probably killed Father Bernado. I found him dead in the parish house a little while ago. They were probably angry at him for not telling them about the other gold in the beginning."

"Bernado morto! Bad, Signor. I help you. We get gold for Italiani. No Americani, no partigiani, no Fascisti. Okay?"

I nodded. And he explained that he would go get a car and find some men to accompany us. Then he took me into a big paneled room with beams in the high ceiling. It looked like an arsenal with all kinds of guns, explosives, and ammo—stuff probably dropped by American and English planes to partisans during the past year. And I wondered as I gazed around how many caches like this existed all over the north. He thrust weapon after weapon into my hand, German, American, Italian, even Russian. And he laughed as I clumsily handled each one. Maybe after all the running and hiding here was someone I could trust. I went to sleep that night in this strange new home not asking any questions about where his wife or family or friends might be, just grateful for the bed and the wine and pasta, the quiet and the security. Temporary as everything might be.

Chapter 14

We set out for Lake Orta at six the next morning. It was misty and cold. Two men were with Giulio, both partisans from the Fifty-second Garibaldi Brigade. One was Aldo Pasquali, a slight, jumpy, talkative, unnerving guy. The other was Pietro Campo, stocky, phlegmatic, stone-faced. They made a good duo, one to get you to relax your guard with a lot of chatter and the other to move in and finish you off in silence. Each one carried a French 9mm machine pistol similar to the one that Valerio used to kill Mussolini, and a huge knife in a sheath. Giulio had no weapon, at least none he wore out in the open.

"Bodyguards?" I smiled at him.

"Si, there are no soldati, no polizia where we go. Briganti dovunque, holding up people, shooting people, kidnapping. We have no trouble. Everybody know me, Aldo Pietro. They no try to capture us."

"A lot of executions going on like the one Saturday?"

"Si, it is bad, Signor. You talk to Fascisti and somebody see you and tell partigiani. They say you against il popolo, and they shoot you. They shave heads of women and march them through streets and then bang, bang. No buono. I say cattivo. Nobody listen. Everybody want to kill Fascisti. They say it is liberazione. Bad, very bad."

"Looks like you've either got a revolution or a civil

148

war brewing up here."

"That is why Communisti want gold. But they do not want people to know. No vote for men who steal, murder, rape. Only capitalists steal, murder, rape, no?" He looked at me funny. So did the two men in the back seat of the Fiat. I couldn't tell whether they were serious or smiling.

We drove down the lake through familiar towns and past 18-century villas and terraced gardens on the hillsides, castles and towers, churches and ruined forts, all ghostly in the mist and semidarkness. Then at Cernobbio we veered west into the mountains onto a dirt road.

"We don't go through Como?"

"No. Molti Americani, Communisti, polizia. They stop us, ask questions, make us show passes. We no find capitano and gold. Okay?"

For a while we were silent up front as the car climbed into the rocky area. Aldo jabbered away in back, sometimes laughing, sometimes shouting at Pietro, his hands going. Even Pietro, whom I had tagged as the laconic type, broke out with a few words. All I could gather from their conversation was that they were eager to see the Fascist tesoro and were wondering how much there would be. They sounded like novice prospectors with gold fever rather than soldiers setting out to recover a lost treasure for their country. Guilio acted keyed up for the expedition too. And I thought to myself, Christ, they think I'm going to lead them to wealth and fame, not death and danger. The damn fools! How simple can you be?"

Or were they so simple? Was I the fool and the naive one? Were they taking me up into the mountains to dispose of me without a witness around? The two in back kept their machine pistols on their laps. And Giulio driving was evasive about the route. The terrain got steeper and wilder and the road narrower and more precipitous, the drop on a couple of turns straight down into a bottomless abyss of rocks and trees. And the towns were small and thinly populated. Snow-capped peaks everywhere.

"How far?" I asked.

"Forty, fifty chilometri, one, two hours. We go slow. Be careful. No one stop us. No Tedeschi, Americani, briganti. Amici."

As we passed through the mountain villages, the isolated settlements on the hills, the farms, Giulio waved to everyone watching and they waved back. Peasants stood in the doorways, in the fields, outside of churches and cafes, calling out to him, "Viva Giulio, viva Giulio!"

"They like you."

"Si, I help them. I chase Tedeschi. I bring food, give protection. They owe me molto, molto. It is very good, no, Signor? I am no hero, but I do good things for people. They thank me. They think I am great man."

"Are you sad now that the war is over and all of this is finito?"

"Tutto finito? Ah, Signor, no, the beginning, the beginning. We fight now the men who have the gold. Always enemies. Old ones turn into new ones and you defeat them and more come. Nothing is over till you are dead. But we are not dead. We get gold. We help Italia. Capisce?"

"Do you think we can get help from the people around Lake Orta?"

"Molti partigiani. They know Giulio. They help. Do not worry, Signor. Who has the gold we shoot."

I was becoming a little skeptical of his bravado. It wasn't anything I could put my finger on, just a suspicion of where his real loyalties lay, what his real aims were. I remembered how he had run into me in Dongo, a little too conveniently to be completely accidental. And yet he acted straight forward enough, and I couldn't detect any deviousness on his part. If he had wanted to, he and Pietro and Aldo could have gotten rid of me back there on one of those treacherous mountain roads.

We reached Gozzano at the southern tip of the Lake at two o'clock, had pasta and a glass of wine in a cafe, then started up the western side of Orta to the Villa Carlotta about two kilometers away where I told them that I had stayed and where the Communists or the capitano or whoever had the gold might be staying. I suggested that he send Aldo and Pietro to survey the house before we approached. He agreed, and they went off while we pulled over into the trees and waited. An hour later they returned to announce the place was deserted. No vehicles, no guards, no signs of anybody. Everything was closed up tight. They even looked in the windows and found the rooms vacant.

Somehow, though, they didn't convince me. If D'Alessandro was alive and had taken the gold, this is where he would have to come. Out of the war, close to Genoa, friendly territory. I had to see for myself. After all I knew the villa and could tell if it had been used recently. Not that much could have changed in the few days I had been gone.

So we drove down the dirt road through the woods to the big house about fifty feet above the lake, parked in front of the garage and got out, each of us with a gun ready. Breaking in the front door, we found everything as Aldo and Pietro had reported. No sign that a soul had been here since the night we left. Some of our ammo cases lay piled up in one corner of the front room still untouched. Dishes on the dining room table reminded me of that last supper. There was even a wine bottle and a candle. I couldn't get over how everything was exactly the way we left it Wednesday night. Uncanny. I even expected D'Alessandro, Carlo, and Bruno to enter and sit down to eat. Except for one thing.

A faint odor hung in the air. We looked at each other wondering what it was, where it came from. We searched the first floor and then went upstairs. The bulb in the hall still shed a dim light when I turned it on, evoking once more that last night in this grim place. I walked down to the room where the captain shot the major. The door was open. Inside face down on the bare floor in front of the canopied bed lay D'Alessandro, Carlo, and Bruno. They were on their stomachs, hands tied behind their backs, shot neatly in the head.

"Christ!" I said, staring at the bodies seeming so unreal stretched out in the dusky light coming from the windows. Except for the major it was the first time I had ever seen Americans in uniform dead.

The three of them confronted me, not moving. Looking down at the corpses, aware of the smell in the air, I tried to speak but nothing came out. All that registered was a constricting dryness in the throat and a hard nausea at the pit of my stomach. What struck me most aside from the unnaturalness of the sight was the absence of any struggle and the cleanness and orderliness of the slaughter. Hardly any blood on the floor.

"Communisti?" I finally spoke.

"No, Signor. I never see men killed in Italia like this."

"Tedeschi? Briganti?"

He shook his head. "Very bad. Strano."

"The captain must have brought the stuff here just as I suspected and somebody jumped him. Maybe he made a deal with the Communists for some of the loot and they followed him here and took it back."

"Bad, Signor, very bad."

"Well, what do we do?"

"We look outside before it is dark. Then we sleep downstairs. And in the morning we tell polizia. Okay?"

"You mean you want to stay here tonight?"

"You afraid, Signor?" He smiled at me.

"I saw the head of my mission, a major, killed in this

152

room just last week. Those guys did it too. You're damn right I'm scared. I'd rather go over to the island, San Giulio, and sleep in the basilica. At least we'd be safe there. Whoever did this could be around in the woods somewhere watching. And we could end up on the floor with these bastards."

He shook his head and we went downstairs and out through the terraced rock garden past evergreens and cypresses to the iron fence, the beach, the boathouse. There was a boat tied up, the same one Salvatore and Giorgio had used to row out and dispose of the major's body.

"Okay," I said, "see that island out there, that's San Giulio." I pointed up the lake to a small plot of land with a campanile rising above a cluster of buildings and trees and the high white wall of a seminary in the background. "The priests are friendly, or they were a couple of months ago. They'll remember me. We hid in the attic over the sacristy to get away from the Tedeschi when we first parachuted here."

"Si, buono, buono. Priests are friendly. But first, Signor, we look. Possible we miss something. The gold, no?"

So we trooped back to the villa through the garden and searched the garage and the grounds and then the house again. There were tire tracks and footprints, empty 9mm shells, and in the kitchen old copies of *Corriere della Sera*. Otherwise nothing was different about the place—gloomy high-ceilinged rooms with spare dark furniture and a few oil portraits, empty wine bottles, dirty dishes.

The captain and his gang couldn't have been here long before they got hit. They couldn't even have had time for a meal. No sign of sleeping bags either. Their weapons and packs gone. They must have been totally surprised. Either the murderers had been hiding inside waiting for them or they pretended to be friends, maybe even partners come to divide the loot. But who were they? That's what disturbed me. And where were they now? Could it be some local gang?

"You know Colonel Valerio, the one who shot Mussolini?" I asked Giulio after we finished our thorough search of the whole place and were sitting in the big bare room overlooking the garden.

"Si, I know him. Non buono. I try to stop him from killing Fascisti at Dongo. He not listen. Pedro, too, try to stop him. Like Communisti he know only one way—kill, kill. The more die the better he like. CLNAI in Milano they not understand the people. Communisti not understand."

"What about Colonel Gentile?"

"I never meet him. I hear of him."

"He was after the gold too. And he got it away from me in Milano and then tried to kill me so that I wouldn't talk. He could be behind this. He learns about the deal the Communists in Dongo make with the captain, or maybe he's part of it, and he comes after him. Or it could be they make a deal and then doublecross him, all the time planning to follow him here to kill him. That way the Party has the whole Fascist tesoro and nobody talks."

"Very bad, Signor, very bad. We go to San Giulio tonight the way you say. Subito."

The only thing I couldn't figure out was how the captain had found out about the gold I left behind. He was chasing me. Unless he had a contact among the Commies who told him what happened in Milan. So then he returns to Dongo, sees Renaldi or somebody in the Party, strikes a deal, his silence for several hundred million, and then heads for Orta after stopping to kill Bernado. But why let the captain come here unless it was a convenient place to dispose of him? In any case, I thought we'd better get the hell out of the area before it was too late. If they had gone to all this trouble to kill D'Alessandro, Carlo, and Bruno, why wouldn't they finish the job by eliminating me, the only remaining one

154

who could pin everything on the Party?

We set off for the island at dusk. Evening falling fast and the chill penetrating. Pietro and Aldo rowed, Giulio sat in the stern, I brooded in the bow, my eyes on the tall companile still visible in the hazy gray atmosphere as if rising out of the water. A few lights dotted the buildings.

About half a mile from shore the two partisans stopped rowing and we hung in the stillness as if suspended. At first I thought they were responding to a boat somewhere. Turning around, I started to ask what was the matter and found guns pointing at me. Although their expressions were unclear in the twilight, their motionlessness and their silence were unmistakable.

"So you guys are in on it too, huh? You dirty bastards! Getting me out here in the middle of nowhere and dumping me. I should have suspected when you spotted me so easily in Dongo that you had something like this in mind."

They still didn't say anything. And I waited for their machine pistols to go off any moment, bullets ripping into my gut. The water slopped against the sides, the oars dripped, the boat creaked. No breeze stirred. Yet I was shivering as if I were naked. And I thought of Mussolini outside the Villa Belmonte, of the major on the canopied bed just before D'Alessandro pulled the trigger. And, Christ, of those times facing the partisans on the way to Milan from Como with the bodies and the gold.

"Well, what are you waiting for?" I continued to stare at them through the haze.

Still not a sound. The three sat rigid before me and grew more and more blurry in the deepening half-light. Like hooded figures. I didn't move either for some strange reason, waiting, numb. A rope dropped over me and tightened around my chest, pinning my arms. The harder I struggled to free myself the tighter the grip

155

became. The plan was clear. Shoot me and bury the body in a bag on the bottom where it could never be found. And not a soul to cry out to, not a boat anywhere, lights very distant. Just bleak hills and a watery grave.

I jerked hard to the right, rocking the boat, and leaped overboard. Guns barked, bullets zinging around me. Diving deeper and deeper, kicking with all my might, I slipped out of the rope that had become slack, almost bursting from holding my breath so long.

Luckily, they had no light to spot me when I surfaced a hundred or so feet away. They were still firing wildly in every direction, hollering, beating the water with oars, the racket rebounding against the hills. But no one plunged in after me. And once I shed my shoes and jacket I began to swim back toward the villa, thinking they would naturally assume I was headed for the island since it was closer and safer and I knew the priests.

My breast stroke, though slow, made little noise and conserved strength. It was hard going at first with clothes on. Behind me oars still splashing and an occasional shot popping through the air. Then an ominous silence with the boat moving farther and farther away. Like a buoy bobbing up and down in the water.

A hundred yards from the beach I looked up. A light shone downstairs in the villa like a pinpoint in the impenetrable blackness. Treading water for a moment, I began to feel a chilling sensation as if suddenly all the cold and fear that I had been forgetting in the anxiety of the moment started needling me. What to do now? Where to go? Too tired to stay out here afloat much longer. The biting air penetrating every nerve end of my toes and fingers, my body stiffening.

It had to be Gentile. He must be working with Giulio. Both of them trying to stop me from reaching the Allies with my story of the gold. Save it and Italy for the Reds.

I stretched out once more and pulled and frog-kicked

with all my might toward the shore, aching, freezing, feeling myself becoming heavier and slower with every stroke. Sinking and swearing to keep on swimming. Not giving up and pushing myself harder and harder toward the dark shoreline.

Chapter 15

Out of the water above the villa I dashed shivering into the woods. The trees and vegetation dense and the ground rough under my stocking feet. Cautiously picking my way to the edge of the clearing, I made for the villa, sticks crackling, leaves rustling. Two jeeps and a weapons carrier were parked in front of Guilio's car. The Fifth Army at last. Thank God!

I ran to the house and looked inside, and there was Captain Donato from SI and Lieutenant Fusco from OG and several sergeants and Italian civilians standing around acting as if they had just arrived. All armed. The Florence Detachment of OSS. Now they could seize Pastore and his paesani when they came in from the lake. No doubt they had discovered the corpses upstairs and were wondering what was going on, whose car that was parked in the drive.

Donato was the first to greet me, a dark, heavyset paratrooper, small eyes, thick lips, bull neck. A veteran of partisan warfare in the Dolemites and Yugoslavia. He had spent two months on the island of Vis with Tito. He looked grim. So did Fusco beside him, taller, lighter skin, a hard mouth and scarred face. Both men had been in the Spanish Civil War, volunteers in the Abraham Lincoln Brigade. Good friends of D'Alessandro.

"Where the hell have you been, Del Greco?" the captain scrutinized me as I walked in.

"Swimming in the lake. What does it look like? Some Commies from Dongo tried to give me a cement bath. But I didn't sink. They've stolen the Fascist treasury, worth half a billion dollars. I had my hands on part of it and then lost it to the bastards in Milan. D'Alessandro tried to grab a share too, but as you've no doubt found out he didn't succeed. He killed the major by the way. There's been a hell of a lot of that sort of thing going on up here this past week."

"The men who took you out on the lake killed Mike, Carlo, and Bruno?"

"No, but I'm sure some of their friends did. Ironic too since the captain blew McGregor's head off last week in that very room and then dumped the body in the lake. A great end to the war up here all right. The bodies are stacking up like at the end of a tragedy."

"It's a gruesome sight. I still don't get what's been going on."

"It's simple. First, the captain kills the major to get a crack at the gold Mussolini is carrying when he leaves Milan last Wednesday. Then he's kaput. I get my hands on the stuff, and they come after me. I think I take care of them with a grenade on the road to Milan and have the gold set to deliver to the Allies when the Commies trick me. But I hear a rumor there's more of the Fascist treasury back in Dongo and go to find it, get ambushed, and some partisans pretending to be friendly end up trying to drown me. Capeesh? You can grab them when they row in. They're still out there hunting for me. I took a real death dive but survived. How do I look?"

"Hey, take it easy, Del Greco," the captain said. "You're still not making too good sense. You better change before you explain any more. You'll catch pneumonia."

"Yeah, I better. Got anything I can wear?" One of the civilians handed me first a towel to dry off and then underwear, a shirt, trousers, socks, shoes, and a jacket that I put on as I talked. Nothing fitted, but at least it was all warm and dry.

"You guys better get down to the boathouse and catch those bastards out on the lake when they come in. It's a Commie plot all right."

"What kind of plot? What are you talking about?" the captain continued to stare hard at me.

"To take over North Italy. That's the reason for the murder of the major and for shooting Mussolini and the Fascists at Dongo, and for stealing the gold too. They want to form a Goddamn Red government up here with Togliatti at the head. And they'll do anything to get it. You saw how they took care of D'Alessandro, one of their own. Talk about your atrocities and war crimes. Not that those guys didn't deserve it."

"Got any idea where Mussolini's gold is now?"

"I'm pretty sure they brought part of it here from Dongo, at least as much as the Reds would let them have. There must have been some kind of deal. Then they were doublecrossed."

"You say you had your hands on some of it."

"That's right, five cases full of jewelry, gold bullion, foreign currency, lire. Quite a chunk of the half billion Mussolini was supposed to be carrying."

"Where is it now?"

"Search me. Maybe in Milan, maybe Como, maybe back in Dongo. I was told a Communist named Renaldi took some of it to Como. But you know, Captain, worse than all that is the fact that some guys in OSS actually seemed to be in on the scheme. Obviously D'Alessandro and his crew were. You could tell that right from the beginning of the Pontiac mission. They were out to take care of the major. And then there's this Captain Silvio in Milan. He's in OSS too. He ends up telling me the gold doesn't exist, it's all my imagination. Jesus, after I had my hands on it. There seems to be a group in the organization working with the Commies,

160

not to liberate the country but to steal it blind."

"You turning in a report like that to Florence?"

"To Florence, Caserta, Washington, you name it. I'm going to the top with this thing. Everybody's going to know what's been happening up here and the real reason for Mussolini's quick execution and the loss of his treasury."

"So you've got it all figured out."

"You're right. The gang in OSS wanted the dough to bring back to the States and start a new racket or something and the Reds wanted it to get the Red machine rolling in high gear. And, boy, I bet it's rolling now. I bet in a couple of weeks, maybe days, those guys will be pasting Red stars in the sky all over northern Italy. And there's nothing the Fifth Army or the Twelfth Air Force can do to stop them."

The group crowded around me in the dining room as I talked, and I thought of the major here last week choking and coughing and Carlo and Bruno and the partisans standing at the foot of the bed while the captain blasted his head off.

"Signor," the stouter of the two civilians spoke to me softly, "you do not tell this. It is bad for amicizia di partigiani e Americani. We help Allies. We kill Mussolini e Fascisti for justice, not gold, for Italia, not Party. We do not want Red state. We do not kill Americani upstairs."

"You're a Communist, aren't you?"

"Si."

"Who did it then? The Christian Democrats, the Socialists? They shot the three of them?"

"Possibile."

"You're either naive or you're lying. And when those guys come in from the lake, you'll find out I'm telling you the truth. It's a power grab, that's all it is, killing Il Duce and taking his gold. I know. I was there. I saw all of it. The people at Dongo didn't want to execute him and his ministers. They didn't want a bloody revenge. It

161

was only the Commies who did. And, of course, some of you guys who figured to take home a couple of million apiece."

"No, no, Signor. We not kill Mussolini for gold. We kill him for justice, for liberazione, for il popolo." His voice rose, his hands started to wave his face flushed.

"I know what I'm talking about. And I can verify everything I've said. Wait till those bastards come in from the lake and you question them. You're going to question them, aren't you?"

I studied the circle of faces gazing curiously at me, set and unsmiling.

"Look, Del Greco," the captain said, "you're tired. Why don't you go upstairs and rest. Then Giovanni will fix you some tasty C-rations. We've got wine too. You probably haven't had a decent meal in days. How about it?"

"Okay, but I'm leaving here right after I eat. You gotta give me a jeep or weapons carrier. I want somebody to do something about what's happening up here. The Red brigades and the Russians could take over this whole goddamn country if we don't do something. And then this whole war would have been for nothing. Do you realize that? For nothing!"

"Calm down now," the captain said.

"Calm down. Christ, do you know what I've been through, what I've seen?" I glared at him.

The two sergeants grabbed me as I started to go toward him. I broke free for a moment and faced everybody.

"What is this?" I turned on the group. "What the hell's going on? Not you guys too? Jesus, my own outfit!"

"We just want you to take it easy, Del Greco," the captain gazed at me. "You've been through a lot these past few days. You're beginning to hallucinate."

"Hallucinate? No, I'm fine. I just need some rest and a little to eat. Then I'm ready to take off, that is if you

162

guys will let me."

"We can't let you leave the villa for a while. You could cause a lot of trouble between the Allies and the partisans with your charges. People in high places might start wondering what's been happening up here and we'd have a hell of a mess on our hands. We've got to go slow in this transition period between war and peace. We don't want to offend anybody we might need."

"You mean this period between war and revolution. So you're keeping me here under guard, that it?"

"Just for a couple of days, until you simmer down and the situation in northern Italy settles. Everything is too tense right now. A spark could set off an ugly confrontation between us and the partisans. And a lot of innocent people could be killed."

"What if I try to escape?" There was silence. They stared at me.

"We won't have any choice then."

"To do what?"

"Just don't try anything, that's all."

"Hey, what is this? You guys in with the Commies too? Sure, of course. You were in Spain with D'Alessandro, weren't you? I should have known."

"We have instructions from headquarters."

"Headquarters didn't send you up here to get me. Don't give me that bull. You guys came for the gold, didn't you? You came to meet D'Alessandro because you thought he had it. He got in touch with you and said to meet him here. Only somebody beat you to it. Now you've got to get rid of me. Am I right?"

One of the sergeants belted me in the stomach, and I doubled up and puked. Then something like a hammer hit me on the head and I went down on my knees and out. But before losing consciousness I could hear Donato saying, "Take him to the lake and shoot the son-of-a-bitch. He's trouble. Then get rid of the body."

When I woke up, I was lying on the beach, the water lapping at the shore. It was still dark. Two dim forms hung over me. I kept still. One poked me with a gun. Another listened to my breathing. There was nothing to do but lie quiet and hope somehow to catch them off guard. The vigil went on, the two sergeants watching and waiting for me to wake up. I felt cold and wet again. I couldn't understand why they hadn't already finished me off. It seemed so useless just to keep me a prisoner like this.

Finally, one left for the villa. The sound of the gate closing and his tramping up the garden path filled the night air. The other one, bigger and clumsier, straightened up and towered over me. From far out on the lake came the splash of oars. The sergeant turned as if to try to spot the boat approaching. When he moved, I grabbed his ankles, tripped him up, and scrambled for the gun he dropped. Before he could recover from the fall and realize what was happening, I whacked him on the top of the head as hard as I could with the butt of the Thompson machine gun. He collapsed with a muffled groan. After searching through his pockets for keys, I took off.

First down the beach and then up through the woods and around to the vehicles in the drive. The others were coming out of the villa and marching through the garden, six indistinct figures moving single file along the path and moving fast, talking loud, shouting to the sergeant on the beach.

Quickly, I moved among the vehicles trying to find one the keys fitted. It was a jeep. I jumped in, turned the ignition, put my feet on the clutch and accelerator, shifted into reverse, and took off. Backing up with a jolt and then swerving around and blasting along the dirt road toward the north-south highway that paralleled the lake. Behind, guys were hollering and firing and after a half a mile the roar of the weapons carrier bore down on me faster and faster.

Where I was going I wasn't certain. And I didn't dare stop and ask directions. Besides, there wasn't anybody around anyway. So the darkness and the strangeness of the terrain made me decide just to keep on following the road as long as I could and maybe reach Florence somehow or find someone not involved in this conspiracy.

There was no question in my mind now that it was a conspiracy hatched in OSS to obtain the gold. Even though I had messed the whole thing up for them, they still had to silence me before it was too late and the plot came out in the open. Still, how did Pastore from Dongo fit in? Why didn't he turn me over to the people trying to kill me in the town? Why did he bring me all the way here? Unless he thought maybe that I was in league with D'Alessandro. And he wanted the gold for himself, and didn't want to share it with the party. Then when he reached Orta and found it was gone, he decided to dispose of me so I couldn't expose him as part of the theft and the murders. He could maybe get in trouble not only with the law but also with the Party if they discovered that he was after the gold himself, possibly even tied in with D'Alessandro some way.

So again it was what to do? Go back up to Dongo instead of down to Florence and blow the whistle on Donato and the Communists up here. Maybe prevent some more deaths. But that could be risky if the people there were connected with the conspiracy.

Then it hit me. Bruna. She would know. And she still must be in town. Didn't she tell me it was her home? I hadn't seen her in Como with the captain when he came after me. Of course, she could be dead too by now like everybody else who had any knowledge of the robbery. But she was tough and resourceful, a child of Italy's terrible years.

So I kept on blasting through the darkness searching for a familiar road sign—Gozzano, Borgomanero, Novara, Milano. Figuring somewhere along the route to the city there ought to be a sign to Como. Almost no traffic. The weapons carrier began fading farther and

165

farther behind me until there wasn't a sound of a motor anywhere. Shadowy hills and fields, orchards and vineyards. Little towns with narrow streets. The headlights beaming against stone walls and green shutters and then tunneling through the country blackness as buildings melted away into the landscape. I figured that I ought to be there by morning, though I was beginning to fight sleep and hunger and exhaustion and the cold all at once.

A Fifth Army convoy coming in the opposite direction stopped me. The major in command wondered what an Italian up here was doing driving a jeep. And I had to pull out my dog tags and explain about OSS and the Pontiac mission.

"Funny," he said, a tall, long-faced, slouching Texan with a soft voice, "we just met another group from OSS down the road in a weapons carrier. The captain said they were hunting German deserters. You with them?"

"Oh, yeah, Captain Donato. How many did he have with him? We split up in several groups."

"Just two sergeants and a lieutenant."

"How far down the road?"

"Maybe eight kilometers. At a crossroads. There's a sign that says Milano. You can't miss it, though they're parked to the left pretty far out of sight. We almost went by without seeing them. You OSS guys are sneaky bastards."

"Goes with the business. Any other road to Milan?"

"No, that's the only one around here we've found. You headed there?"

"No, I'm supposed to go to Como."

"Well, try the next left. Goes over to Sesto Calende, then I think there's a road to Varese that's not too far from Como. The First Armored is there now. Maybe they can help you. You looking for deserters too?"

"Yeah, kind of." I thanked him and shot past a line of jeeps and weapons carriers and two-ton trucks, waving as I went by at the helmeted GI's in battle

166

jackets holding MI's and looking sleepy and cold in the headlights. The turn was only a short mile away, and I took it and drove a little farther on until I felt myself dozing off and the jeep zigzagging from side to side. I pulled up in an orchard and slumped down and went to sleep despite everything—the damp clothes, my empty stomach, the freezing weather, and Donato and his bushwhackers.

Chapter 16

Como looked a lot more friendly than it did the last time I was here with Scala. People on the streets shopping and gathering in groups to talk. GI's with First Armored Division triangular patches on their shoulders mingling with the crowd. Police and carabinieri patrolling and directing traffic. An end-of-the-war holiday fervor still hanging in the air. Red and black Communist slogans and emblems splashed on walls. Though you could sense everything returning to normal.

I spotted Division Headquarters and reported to a Major Nash of the Sixth Armored Infantry and explained who I was and what outfit I belonged to and where I needed to go to complete my mission—Dongo to retrieve secret documents left behind in the town hall where Mussolini and his ministers had been imprisoned. OSS wanted them for the files. Of course, the major, an intelligence officer, knew the organization, didn't he? Oh, yes, he was a good friend of the Major Suhling of the 2677 Regiment D Company at Florence. They had met at Siena. He had even used some of the information supplied by our agents during the rapid advance of the battalion through Brescia and Bergamo. A short, reserved-looking man, salt-and-pepper hair, broad face, glasses, he reminded me of a high school science teacher.

By two o'clock I had a jeep, a tank of gas along with a

couple of give gallon cans to spare, a uniform with Tec sergeant stripes, and a .45 and a carbine. Not to speak of a good meal, the first in a long time. I could have had a driver too if I had wanted. But no, I'd rather go alone. Too many secret documents involved. He understood and handed me travel orders and sent me flying.

It was just in time too. As I was heading out of the city searching for the lake road, I caught a glimpse of Donato and his crew trundling through the narrow streets in their weapons carrier and peering down every alley and into every doorway. Maybe I had an hour's lead on them, maybe less depending on how soon they contacted the major. Or maybe they wouldn't dare go see him, at least not directly and would ask around until they hit on my identity and destination.

A much prettier day to travel up the lake than the last time. Patches of blue sky and bursts of sunlight. The water sparkling and boats drifting along. Azaleas, rhododendrons, and orchards flowering everywhere and filling the air with fragrance. Great white and gray, yellow and pink villas at the water's edge and rows of cypress, cedar, and myrtle. Lush tropical gardens blooming behind delicate old grill work. And in the distance shadowy blue mountains capped with snow looming through the haze. They were Mussolini's last view of the world from where he stood outside the Villa Belmonte if he happened to glance up and gaze out past Valerio's machine pistol. Which I remembered he appeared to do when he told his executioner to fire away in that last flare up of bravado.

People waved in all the towns—Cernobbio, Argegno, Tremezzo, Cadenabbia—and I waved back with a shy liberator's smile. It felt good for a change after so many hair-breadth escapes and so much pressure to be driving along in a jeep in an American uniform, staring at the big-bosomed women in their flowery dresses carrying baskets on their heads and kids already yelling, "Chocolate, joe. Wanna piece of ass?" Gaunt men staring out of doorways. It was the Italy I had always dreamed of—buoyant and picturesque, primitive and sad, an old-world shadow falling across the landscape.

As I drove up the steep hill from Musso once more past Vall'Orba and the fatal blockade, ready to plunge down into the gloomy town, I hesitated for a moment worried about recognition. But I new that I had to make at least one more attempt to recover the gold, at least one more attempt to discover what had happened to it. The thing had become an obsession with me—so many people dead, my life on the line, a Red state up here in the making. If I could locate Bruna and she would talk and we exposed what was going on, I might be able to salvage something from this disastrous mission. Besides, who would recognize me in this uniform? Anyone who did away with me would be taking on the U.S. army.

Nothing had changed about the place and probably never would—the empty square and the war memorial, the low wall along the bay and the public urinal, the town hall with its Norman arch, the narrow streets. Dusk drifting across the stones and over the water evoking the slaughter of last Saturday and the mob standing there waiting for the gunfire to burst and the fifteen to drop. No matter how often I thought of the war—ten, twenty years from now—the ghosts of that cloudy cold evening would always haunt me. There was something about the area and the light that made what had happened here seem almost destined. A natural melancholy hung over the buildings, the barren hills, the lake, gray and chilling and unfathomable.

Father Bernado's replacement, Father Donatello, was a tall, stout man with black hair, a double chin, and small bright eyes. He brought me into the very room where I had last seen the murdered priest. The same crucifix, the same holy pictures and statues, the same wooden desk and straw-bottomed chairs. When I told him that I had known the dead padre, his face darkened and he described the bloody death and the way in which the American captain had used him to hide the Fascist gold.

That is what I had come to see about, sent by the U.S. Army to investigate its disappearance. Some of the cases were taken to Milan with the bodies of those executed in the square last Saturday. But weren't there more cases of gold in the town? Possibly some were even here in the parish house or the church?

"No, no, Capitano. Communisti have gold. They take it to Como. Not here."

"I'm a sergeant."

"Ah, Sergeante. All is gone. Dongo forget war, forget Communisti, forget Fascisti. We have peace, no?"

"How about Father Bernado's death? Did the Communists kill him?"

"No, no, Americani. They afraid he talk about gold."

"Any Italiani with them?"

"No, no Italiani."

"What about Bruna?"

He stiffened and looked intently at me. "You know Bruna?"

"I drove with her in Il Duce's convoy. She said she was helping the American captain. She had five cases containing part of the treasure in her lorry. Is she in Dongo now? I'd like to talk to her. I think she can tell me what finally happened to all the gold that didn't go to Milan. And she could probably tell me who killed Captain D'Alessandro at Lake Orta. He was shot there, he and two other Americans."

"No, she is gone, Sergeante. Niente. She tell you niente."

"You mean she left town because she was afraid to talk to me or to anyone? The Communists have threatened her, too, maybe done away with her?"

"Non capisco, Sergeante. She go far away after

171

Father Bernado is shot."

"Dove?"

"I not know."

"Does that mean then that she could know something about the murder and is afraid to reveal it?"

"Oh, no, no, she know niente, niente." He lowered his head. "Sergeante, it is very hard for her in the war. Capisce? She lose her family. They are all dead. Only Enrico left. Very sad."

"But somebody must know where she's gone."

He shrugged his shoulders and threw up his hands, his whole huge frame shaking.

"I've got to find her. She's the only one left who can begin to clear up this mess. Can't you ask somebody in town where she might be? People know her here."

"You put her in prison?"

"No, no, I just want to ask her a few questions. Not only about the gold and the capitano but also about the murder of Father Bernado. Capisce, Padre?"

He nodded, his massive face with the tiny eyes embedded in sallow flesh becoming solemn, wrinkled, dark.

"Communisti after you?"

"Maybe."

"Americani?"

"Si."

"They come to Dongo?"

"They might if they find out in Como I'm up here. They don't want me to tell what's been going on. I think they were involved with the capitano in trying to take the Fascist treasury on Saturday. It could be bad, no?"

He continued to study me with that fat, immobile face.

"Si, si," he suddenly lit up. "You come. I show you something. You help."

Moving toward the door, his great Chaucerian hulk shaking, he asked me to follow him upstairs and along a dusky corridor to a semidarkened room with two

172

narrow windows. On the bed against the wall and barely visible in the light lay Bruna staring at the ceiling. She sat up startled when she realized we were there. A shapeless brown dress, bare feet, long black hair down her back. So different from the other day when she had it tucked under her cap. Thin legs and big braless breasts with the nipples obvious. None of that tomboy quality that I remembered so well from the convoy, except for the sharpness of the expression and the intense way she faced me after her initial fear faded.

Neither of us spoke for a moment. The priest left the room without closing the door. She put her feet on the stone floor and stared up at me.

"You hiding from the Communists or the Americans?" I finally broke the silence.

"I hide from you, Signor," she said in a strained, husky whisper.

"From me?"

"Si, you know about the gold. You come back to find it like the capitano. Non buono. Morte, morte."

"And I was supposed to be killed like him, too, wasn't I, at Lake Orta?"

"Si."

"Why?"

"They afraid you tell the Allies about tesoro and the partigiani have to give it up. Molti, molti lire. Very big, very important to Party. Capisce, Signor?"

"You were in on the whole thing from the beginning, weren't you?"

"Si, Enrico and I. We Communisti. I lie to you. We go with capitano to make sure partigiani get gold, not Americani. Father Bernado help too."

"But he let me take the cases."

"He afraid of Salvatore and Giorgio. They kill him. You trick him. Capitano angry when he find out. He go after you and he come back and say he hear there are more cases and he want them. He kill Father Bernado so he not talk. He mad at him too. And he take gold to

Lake Orta."

"Not all of it, though. Luigi Renaldi got most of it for the Party, didn't he?"

"Ah, si. But capitano get molti lire. He say he must have molti lire or he tell Allies what partigiani do. They afraid of him."

"So that's why they killed him at Lake Orta, not just to get back the lire they gave him but to keep him quiet."

"It is true. A very bad man, Signor. He try to, what you say, rape me. Enrico stop him." She stared at the floor, her face screwed up tight, her hands clasped together. Suddenly she looked so young, so helpless, and I had always thought of her as tough and experienced.

"His friends in OSS came to see him at Orta, thinking he had part of the treasury. They tried to kill me the way Pastore did. Now they're on their way here. Maybe they'll be looking for you too."

"Me?"

"They're after anybody who can tell them where the gold is, who killed the captain, and who can involve them in this mess."

"I do not know where the gold is. You help me?"

"I'll do the best I can. How did you ever get mixed up with all of this anyway?"

"They tell me I help partigiani, I join Party and do away with Fascism. Buono. Americani come, non buono. Padre killed. I am afraid, Signor." She hesitated. "Victor." She slid off the bed and stood close to me. It was the first time she had used my name. There was a terribly vulnerable look about her, the long hair, the oval face puffy and hurt, the bare feet. Then without any warning she threw her arms around my neck and kissed me on the lips. Shocked, I stood stiff, slowly embracing her, drawing her hard against me until I felt her body yielding with incredible softness and sensuality, the lips, the thighs, melting into me. I put my tongue inside her mouth.

"Americani, Americani!" the priest burst into the room, shouting and spitting out Italian at too rapid a rate for me to comprehend. We broke the embrace.

"What's he saying?"

"Americani in piazza and ask about you," Bruna translated. "A lorry and four men. They say you are wanted as deserter. We hide you."

"No, I better leave. If I don't, they'll come here looking for me and harm you both. They know I've got the goods on them. They're in this whole thing with the captain. And they could force you to talk, Bruna. Even kill you." She looked strangely at me.

"I find Enrico and partigiani," she said. "They help. They have guns. They protect you."

"Okay, fine. Round up as many as you can. But don't let them go to the square and kill the Americans. There's been enough of that. It could get me, you, and the whole town in a lot of trouble."

"Padre help you. They no harm him." She glanced at the stout man towering over us, his face flushed.

"Si, Sergeante, I help you."

We walked downstairs and through the house to the street and the jeep. It seemed darker and colder out than ever. A raw dampness in the air. Bruna vanished instantly, noiselessly. Not a sound anywhere. This creepy place was getting on my nerves again.

"I better not wait until she gets back. It might be too late."

"They shoot you, Sergeant?"

"They could. They tried before. I suppose from their standpoint I am a deserter. I could betray them."

"Partigiani take them prisoner."

"No, that would be bad. Then you'd have the whole First Armored Division up here. They'd reduce this town to rubble. I'll try to slip by them somehow. I don't want any of you involved. They might try to seize Bruna. You help her, Padre?"

"Si, si. You too. You hide in church."

"No, I've got to get out of Dongo. I can't stay around here any longer. Too much is at stake."

I hopped in the jeep and started for the piazza. The headlights filled the little drab streets, brightening the windows and doors and shining on the cobblestones. If they couldn't hear me coming, they must be dead or gone. The sound of the motor in first gear shook the buildings to their foundations and reverberated through the town as if a convoy were passing through the place.

Chapter 17

At the entrance to the piazza I stopped and cut off the motor and the lights. A weapons carrier with a canvas back stood silhouetted along the low wall. Nobody around it. Not a person anywhere. The only sound the slapping of the water against the jetty and the whine of the wind off the lake. I thought of Scala in that green car flashing his lights, of the fifteen Fascists lined up to be mowed down.

The best thing to do was to wait for Bruna and her brother and the partisans. But what if they never arrived? And if they did come, what if they were in league with Donato in some way? I could be threatened from both front and rear. So I decided to make a quick break for it, hit the lake road and head south before they realized what was happening.

Suddenly I heard someone coming, a faint footfall.

"Victor," a low voice called out. I pulled out my .45, still keeping an eye on the weapons carrier and expecting any moment for bodies to leap out and begin firing.

Bruna slipped up beside me and put a hand on my arm.

"I not find Enrico and partigiani. You go."

"What about Americani? Are they out there waiting for me?"

"Si, they wait for you. They know you go to Como tonight."

"So the bastards are sitting out there instead of hunting for me in town."

"That is what I hear."

"Then somebody must have told them I was around and what I planned to do. The padre?"

"No, no, I think, Victor, someone see your jeep outside the church. They tell Americani. Get molti lire. Capisce?"

I gripped the wheel, staring out into the blackness, wondering how the hell I was ever going to get out of this trap.

"I go with you, no?" She tightened her grip on my arm.

"You afraid to stay here?"

"Si. They know I am your friend."

"But I'm not a Fascist. They can't accuse you of collaboration with the enemy, shave your head."

"No, no. But you take gold to Milano, give to Allies. You do not want Il Duce shot."

"You mean I'm not a Communist?"

"Si."

"But I couldn't take you with me now. Not out there. They could kill us both. It's an ambush, I'm certain. We appear and they blast the hell out of us. If there were another way down the lake, okay. But since there isn't, and I've got to reach Como before they get to me, I guess I'll just have to take that chance. But you don't have to. No, you stay here, Bruna."

She sighed. I put an arm around her as she stood beside the jeep. She kissed me on the cheek, not a long kiss, quick and hard and nervous.

"I'm sorry. I wish I could take you with me. Would you be willing to tell all you know about the gold to the Allies?"

"No, I cannot do that, Victor. It would be bad. I go to Como because of you, not because of gold. Capisce?"

"How about it, then, if you hid somewhere? In the

178

church? And I came back here with the army to rescue you?''

"But I cannot talk about the gold." She was silent. "No, no, I stay, you not come back. That is the way war is."

"Yeah, I'm afraid that's the way it is. Still I might come back anyway, not to ask you about the gold but to see you as a friend. Okay?"

"Si, okay." Her voice choked up.

I got out of the jeep and hugged her hard against me, practically lifting her off the stones. Her face was wet with tears, her body shaking. When I let her down, she wriggled out of my arms and disappeared into the darkness. And for a moment I stood watching after her and then turned my attention to the square. A terrible quiet filled the great empty space.

So much had happened out there last week, so damn much that I was almost ready to believe the place was cursed. The whole town in fact. The stillness had such an ominous quality, so suspenseful, so strange. I couldn't even hear a dog bark, a door close, footsteps on the cobblestones in the streets behind me. Time to beat it the hell out of here all right.

I climbed back into the jeep and took a deep breath, switched on the motor, and drove slowly, blindly out into the open area until I reached the lake road to Musso. Abruptly, I shifted into second, went a little way, then pushed the gear into high, turning on the lights and jamming the pedal down hard. The jeep took off like a bronco. Lights from the weapons carrier across the way flooded the night. Machine guns and rifles opened up. I kept on rattling, roaring, bumping over the stones faster and faster toward Vall'Orba at the top of the hill. Bullets banging against the side, one shattering the windshield and throwing glass all over. I almost smashed into the wall on the left and plunged down the steep bank into the lake.

"The bastards," I muttered to myself, "the dirty

179

bastards!" And then my thoughts turned to Bruna. Where would she go in Dongo if she was too scared to return to the church? Should I come back to get her the way I promised? And even if she wanted to go away with them, would she? Could she? What would I do with her? Love her, marry her, persuade OSS to give her money to resettle somewhere? So sad, so frightened, so exhausted like so many people in this ruined country who had suffered from the war.

Nobody followed me once I got to the top of the hill. There wasn't even a barrier set up where the partisans had halted Il Duce's convoy last Friday. But I was ready for them just in case, moving around the great rock cautiously, the .45 in one hand, the carbine on the seat beside me. I at least expected somebody to be up above firing down. Not a shot. They were going to let me escape after all. I couldn't believe it. So down the road I flew like a bat out of hell until my headlights were shining on the chipped enamel Musso sign.

And then it was smooth sailing the rest of the way through the somnolent little settlements along the lake. No more roadblocks or checkpoints, no more crowds in the streets or sound of gunfire. And, I thought, wouldn't it be great to come back here some summer and enjoy the scenery, visit the old villas and churches, ramble over the ruins and through the orchards and vineyards. Just let go in this mellow, sort of melancholy atmosphere.

After a while, though, I began to feel limp. My hands shook at the wheel. My body grew hot despite the cool breeze off the water. I slowed up, coasting down hills and through tunnels, stopping a couple of times to get a grip on myself and keep from collapsing. Finally there were signs for Como and the sight of U.S. army vehicles. In town, GI's walking the streets eyeing the women, the American flag flying, lights and traffic. So different from that dark, abandoned-looking village I had left no more than an hour and a half ago.

Major Nash was surprised to see me. A captain, a lieutenant, and two sergeants, who came through this afternoon searching for me, claimed that I was a deserter. They said they were ordered by OSS to find me. I had run off with top secret papers.

"They're up at Dongo. They tried to kill me all right. You better check on them. They're the ones you should be after, not me. They're looking for Mussolini's treasury that the Commies stole. I tried to get it for the Allies, and I almost succeeded. But they thought I had it or knew where it was and were afraid I'd implicate them in the great gold robbery. Of course, I lied to you about hunting for documents up there. Make any sense?"

He shook his head.

"There was two to five hundred million in that treasury, Major. And everybody and his brother up here was after it."

"That's a lot of money, Sergeant."

"It's not the money I'm interested in anymore, though. Christ, so many have been killed trying to get their hands on it. No, it's the guys behind the mayhem I want to expose. I need to report to Florence as soon as possible, talk to Major Suhling, tell him what's been going on. He's got to go after the damn gangsters in the organization."

I stopped talking and gazed at the major staring hard at me. "My mission is over up here. Everybody who parachuted in with me at Lake Orta last February is kaput." And quickly I told him the story as coherently as I could under the circumstances. He continued to study me in that strange, detached, unnerving way as I meandered and stammered and exaggerated and left out lots of details. All the time sensing myself faltering, going back over phrases, gripping myself, then losing control, struggling to stay conscious and lapsing into longer and longer stretches of blankness.

"You all right, Sergeant? Want to stop here and continue maybe tomorrow or in a couple of hours?"

"I'm kind of dizzy, sir. I don't think I can finish now." Suddenly everything blacked out. At first I fought the loss of consciousness with all my might, tightening my fists, stiffening my legs. It wasn't any good. And the next thing I knew I was in a white bed smelling antiseptic air, staring at blank walls and a blank ceiling. A tall MP with a black armband stood outside the door. The major hovered over me with his long nose and thin lips and bumpy chin.

"Am I under arrest?"

"You fainted. We brought you here to rest and for your own protection. I contacted Major Suhling in Florence and he relayed your story to Colonel Gatling in Caserta. They want you down there right away, as soon as you feel strong enough to travel. You apparently stirred up a hornet's nest with all that stuff you told me."

"About the gold, huh?"

"That and all the murders you reported. Christ, you've been in your own private war up here, Sergeant, you know. You're lucky to be alive."

"What about the Fascist treasury?"

"Nobody claims to know anything about it. The partisans at Dongo say there never was any such thing. So does your good friend Father Donatello. And the CLNAI and the Communists in Milan profess their ignorance of the stuff. General Crittenberger talked to General Cadorna. He had no knowledge of the wealth. And there's not a trace of Captain Donato and the lieutenant and two sergeants. Nobody at Dongo said they saw them. They've just vanished, weapons carrier and all. So have the bodies of Captain D'Alessandro and his two lieutenants that you said were murdered at Lake Orta. We checked on the villa you mentioned. Nobody there."

"What about Captain Silvio and Major Rosselli in Milan?"

"They insist they know nothing about what you've

told me. They thought you were off your rocker, coming there and ranting on about gold, trying to get them off on a treasure hunt. And the Red Colonel, Gentile, we can't locate him. Nobody ever heard of him. What's more, Colonel Valerio says he's never heard of you, never even seen you, and you certainly weren't there when he executed Mussolini. You never drove the bodies of the Fascists to Milan in the furniture van. Your friends, Giuseppe and Mario, are nonexistent, too, as far as the CLNAI is concerned. No record of them. So I guess, Sergeant, it's your word against everybody else's. Tough."

"You believe me, Major? Don't you see it's a cover-up? They've all gotten together to protect someone, hide something. They're being paid off. I'm not making up anything. It all happened exactly the way I said it did. My God, how could I make up all that? It's impossible."

"I'd like to believe you, Sergeant. It sounds convincing. But there's no way you can prove what you say happened with half of the people involved dead or missing and the other half not talking or calling you a liar."

"So I didn't accomplish anything, did I? The whole thing was a waste."

"Oh, maybe you accomplished more than you think."

"I didn't get the gold, though. I didn't stop them from killing Mussolini or Major MacGregor."

"You couldn't do that alone. Don't worry. You had a rough time, but you did all right. The Communists aren't going to take over the country yet." He leaned down and put a hand on my shoulder and smiled. It was a nice fatherly gesture, and I smiled back.

"By the way, there's an Italian girl out in the hall. Says she'd like to speak to you. Name's Bruna. You didn't mention her in your story." He grinned down at me. "Up to seeing her?"

"But I thought—"

"What?"

"Nothing. Yeah, let her come in. She's from Dongo."

"Why don't you ask her if she knows anything about Captain Donato and the men you say were after you? About the gold too. She might have a line on it."

"I'll ask her. Could we talk alone? It's a personal matter. Nothing to do with all this."

"You didn't knock her up, did you?"

"No, nothing like that."

"Okay. But just a few minutes. You're still pretty weak."

"Don't worry. She won't climb in bed with me. I'm not ready for that yet."

"I've never seen a GI who wasn't ready for that when he had the chance, and I've seen 'em in all conditions —legs amputated, their piece hanging by a thread, a nervous wreck. You watch it, son." He smiled.

After he left with the MP, Bruna shuffled in and looked around. A green blouse and brown skirt accentuated her breasts and hips and thin legs. She had never appeared so sexy. It was hard to recall that chunky tomboy in the convoy rolling up the lake that cold rainy morning not too many days ago. Or that sad girl lying on the bed in the parish house, hair down over her shoulders, staring at the ceiling. She came over and stood beside me. I reached for her hand and gazed up into the big dark eyes. Her fingers were wet and limp.

"So you've come to me. I didn't have to go after you. Afraid?"

"Si, I come, Victor. I am afraid."

"They know you're here?"

"I do not know."

"You want to stay? The major will arrange it. He'll find a safe house for you. I'll explain the circumstances to him. Not everything, of course, but enough to make him understand you need protection."

I tightened my grip on her hand. It felt warmer, damper. Her eyes had a pained expression.

"No, I not stay. I go. I come to see you one more time, Victor. It is necessary."

"You mean to say arrivederci for good?"

"Si, arrivederci for good." She didn't focus on me, staring at the white wall as if facing me were somehow too difficult. And I couldn't bear to watch her struggle with the goodbye, the tears, the breaking down.

She withdrew her hand all of a sudden, fumbled a minute with her bag. Instead of a handkerchief she pulled out a small pistol, a Beretta. The sight of the gun was so unexpected, so momentous I froze gaping at the stubby barrel.

"Oh, no, Bruna," I said. "God, not you too now! You can't. You're not one of them. You can't do it to me. I love you. You care for me."

A puzzled look crossed her face. Her hands wavered. The gun, pointed down toward my head, loomed enormous. I had no doubt that she would pull the trigger. She straightened up, stiffened.

"I do it. It is the only way."

"You mean I know too much?"

"Si, we lose everything. That is what they tell me. I am sorry, Victor."

"But my God, you'll lose everything too, won't you?"

"Si."

"They'll hear the shot in the hall. You won't get away. You'll go to prison." Her brown eyes fixed on me, and I could feel myself grow hot all over and perspire terribly. I tried to reach up and deflect the gun, remember the major back at Lake Orta and the captain standing over him with the .45. But there was nothing to do but lay my arm across my face to deflect the bullet when it came. My throat was too constricted, too dry to call out, even to speak in a whisper.

Continuing to concentrate on me without really

185

seeing me, she hesitated, her hand wavering, lowering the muzzle until it was inches away from my forehead. I could already hear the shot, sense everything blacking out, imagine my brains splattering against the pillow. And once more, as it did days ago in Milan when the partisans lined Giuseppe and Mario and me against the wall, my whole life flashed by in one frantic, final second. No sound, just intense silence, a blurry scene.

Still she delayed. Her eyes grew larger, darker, her hand trembled, the gun wavered.

"You can't do it," I managed to utter in a small voice.

She brushed away a desperate thrust to reach up and touch her. I fought to roll over out of bed. The revolver continued to hang there above me as if suspended in midair. The waiting became almost unbearable. Then she dropped it in her bag and walked out of the room, turning her back sharply and never once glancing over her shoulder. The door clicked. Her footsteps tapped down the hall. I flung out my arms and sighed, staring at the white ceiling. The knot in my stomach eased.

After the panic subsided I wanted to get up and run after her, tell her not to go back to Dongo, to stay here with me. I would protect her, the U.S. Army would protect her. She could go to the States to live away from all this. But I couldn't budge.

"Your friend left in a hurry," the major said as he ambled back into the room. "You two have a little quarrel?"

"Did she have a car?"

"Someone was driving her. In fact, there were two men."

"Stop them. They're going to kill her. They sent her here to do a job on me."

"Who? Who sent her? You sure you know what you're saying?"

"Who the hell do you think? The bastards who've been doing all the executing around here these last

186

couple of days."

"My God, Sergeant!"

He rushed out shouting, "Corporal, Corporal, stop that car."

For an hour everything in the room was quiet. I lay still listening for footsteps and watching the light on the walls and the ceiling brighten and fade, the shadows shifting and the white background becoming gray. I thought of home and of all the people whom I had seen die in the past couple of weeks.

"We found her," the major said opening the door. His voice sounded flat.

"Thank God!" I struggled to sit up to greet him and sank back.

"She's dead. They shot her in the head and left the body in a field outside Como on the lake road."

"Goddamn it! The bastards! I knew that's how it would end. The same way it did for the others who took that road to Dongo."

"Sorry, Sergeant." He leaned down and touched me again on the shoulders, unsmiling now.

"She saved my life." I gazed up at him, tears in my eyes.

"I know she did. We found a revolver in her bag. It was loaded. She must have thought a lot of you."

"Or maybe she was just sick of all the killing going on up here. But I don't think she ever loved me. No, it was nothing like that. If we had had a chance to get to know each other better, something might have happened between us. You never can tell. But now—"

"Just a sad memory, huh?"

"No, a good memory, a very good memory, Major. I'll never forget her."

"We're still going to keep a guard on you. They might be back. When you feel better, you can tell me everything you left out. Which I guess was plenty."

"You mean where she fitted in?"

"That and whatever else you can remember."

"I will, but it won't help you get back the gold or stop the Reds up here. They might not take over the government but they're going to make it tough for anybody who does. They're the big winners in this war, Major. The rest of us get shafted."

"You could be right, Sergeant. Now you better rest. You've been in one hell of a war."

"But it doesn't seem the same one you've been in, does it?"

"No, I guess not. Yours has been something special all right."

Chapter 18

Nobody except nurses and doctors came near me for two days after Bruna's death. Not even the major. The MP stayed outside the door. An Italian cleaning woman acted deaf and dumb. It was like living in an isolation ward. I couldn't even write a letter home or contact anybody from OSS or read *The Stars and Stripes*. All that filtered through the screen of silence was the fact that Hitler had committed suicide in his Berlin bunker, the war had ended in Europe, and GI's were talking about going home or to the Far East.

Then late one night two beer-belly MP sergeants— black armbands and yellow hash marks on their sleeves, campaign ribbons on their chests, .45's on their web belts—appeared and told me to get dressed. We were going for a ride. They escorted me to a command car, and we drove through the darkness and into the next day on our way south. Nobody spoke. My protests, my questions pounded against the backs of their hard wrinkled necks. Over the Po, through the rubble of Apennine villages, across the Arno and around the walls of Siena, and down the long hilly road to Rome. Crippled tanks and trucks rusting in the fields, empty ammo boxes stacked up, the broken wing of a plane, a small wooden cross beside the highway. Near Lake Bolsona a towering castle rising up over the wild Etruscan countryside of the dead. Still no word where we were going or why I was being escorted by armed guards. And the possibility of a clandestine execution somewhere in the desolate south crossed my mind as the reticence of the two deadheads deepened and their answers to my questions degenerated from monosyllables to grunts.

Then just below Viterbo they suddenly came alive and stopped for a teen-aged girl in a brown dress walking along the road. She resembled Bruna in a way, short and bosomy with thick black hair and one of those Madonna faces, though pockmarked. She got in back with me, and we pulled off into an olive grove immediately and parked behind a cluster of trees.

"You wanna go first, kid?" the driver turned around and looked at me. He was the stouter and more square-jawed of the two. "Give her a cigarette." It was the first time either of them had spoken to me.

"No thanks. I haven't recovered enough for that. Still kind of weak."

"Hell, it don't take all that much. I bet you ain't had any pussy for a hell of a long time."

"Sorry, I'm just not up to it."

"Okay, then, get out. I'll go first. You get the next crack, Tex." The sergeant with the glasses grunted. "Shit, these fucking people owe us something for fighting their damn war for them."

As I got out, the girl smiled at me and prepared to lie down in the back seat, her knees up and her legs spread apart. She didn't appear to have anything on under the dress. So far she hadn't said a word. All I noticed was the pitted skin, and the bad teeth, the large breasts and the muddy feet. And a rancid odor.

Tex and I went off about a hundred yards to camp behind a tree. While I smoked a cigarette, my first in a long time, he chewed on tobacco and spat frequently. His right cheek bulged with a wad. Standing there reminded me of waiting for someone to go to the toilet.

"Not too hot, kid," the sergeant muttered coming

from the command car buttoning his fly. "You didn't miss nothing." Tex ambled over toward the vehicle, ignoring the remark. "Shoulda saved my butt. I had better in Algiers with an Ayrab. Didn't do nothing. Just give me that silly smile. Stiff as a board."

"Well, what do you want for one cigarette?" I looked at him. He eyed me as if he didn't quite understand, something vaguely menacing in his glance.

We were back on the road in ten minutes. The girl stood on the shoulder gazing after us with a melancholy expression, a cigarette in her mouth.

Nobody spoke the rest of the way except to make a few lewd comments about the women walking down the Via Veneto in the Holy City with their breasts hanging loose and their dresses above their knees and their high cork shoes that set off sexy legs. For all its famous buildings and broad avenues Rome seemed drab and dirty.

The crumbly old palace above Caserta where OSS had its headquarters appeared just as it did in February except for the quonset huts on the cobblestones in front of the statue of Ferdinand IV where peacocks used to strut. Below, the campagna stretched to the Bay of Naples, the big brick Victor Emmanuel Palace and its park with ponds and fountains in the center and Vesuvius to the left smoking away. One of those old-world picture postcard vistas you bring home and put in the attic of your mind and take out thirty years later and think, Jesus, I'd like to go back and see all that again.

I got out of the command car and went into the court-yard and reported to the adjutant on the first floor, a brisk-looking captain with glasses. He assigned me to an officer's villa down the road with instructions not to talk to anyone about my mission. When I asked if I could see Colonel Gatling or Mr. Lewis in SI, he said he was sorry, but they weren't available. In a few days I would be going back to the States.

What the hell was going on? Was I being confined to

191

quarters? Put under a kind of house arrest? He didn't know. He was simply relaying orders from higher up. Sorry.

So I spent the next couple of days climbing the bleak hills behind the villa and trying to figure out how the Fifth Army ever made it through to Cassino and Rome. Or wandering into Caserta and talking to the kids playing soccer and the women washing clothes in a trough in the square. All the time waiting for something to happen, for someone to talk to me about the mission. Anything to break the monotony and the isolation. Officers smiled in the mess, nodded as they passed by on the road and in the villa, probably wondering what a noncom was doing in their quarters. But nobody spoke. That was the strange and maddening thing. As if I were a pariah.

A week went by and no word from anybody. It was worse than being in a North African reppo deppo waiting to be shipped out. At least there you had crap games going and good conversation. Finally, I decided, what the hell, I had to speak to someone, find out something. I wasn't going to remain in this crazy isolation any longer. So I went down to the palace one morning and asked to see Colonel Gatling. The captain in the outer office was brusque. What did I want to see him for? I told him it was about the Pontiac mission. And he should inform the colonel that I knew a lot more than I had revealed to the major up in Como. If he wouldn't see me, I was going to contact Allied Headquarters down the hill and contact somebody in G-2.

The captain talked on the phone and then asked me to wait. I did, for an hour, and then at last walked into an ornate, thronelike room with cherubs painted on the high blue ceiling, gilded furniture, an Oriental rug on the stone floor, a huge fireplace. Behind a leather-top desk sat the colonel in an immaculate uniform, the slicked-down graying hair, the square, stiff shoulders, the reluctant smile, the West Point aplomb. At first he just stared at me as I saluted and stood at attention.

"At ease, Sergeant. Now what is it you want to tell me that's so urgent?"

"First, I want to know what OSS is going to do with me? When am I going to the States?"

"Next week on the first troopship. I'm sorry for all the trouble and the delay. The general's orders. He insisted that you talk to nobody about what happened up North."

"You can't tell me why?"

"I'm afraid only he can do that, Sergeant. Now what is it you've got to tell me that's so new?"

"Will I see him when I get back to the States? Maybe I better wait and give him the information."

"You might, and then again you might not. So why not go ahead and tell me and I can send him a cable?"

"All right, I might as well. I'm suspicious of the real purpose of the Pontiac mission. Aside from supplying the partisans, working as liaison with the CLNAI in Milan, and capturing Mussolini there seemed to be something else. Frankly, I think it was part of some OSS conspiracy that had nothing to do with the war directly and everything to do with stealing Mussolini's treasury. I'm sure Captain D'Alessandro and Captain Donato were involved and maybe even Captain Silvio. You understand what I'm getting at?"

"Sorry, I can't tell you a thing about that. I don't know any more than you do about it, probably not as much. There are some things the general keeps to himself. He doesn't even tell those close to him about them. Evidently the Pontiac mission is one of those things. I have a hunch, though, when you return to Washington, you'll find out what you want to know."

"Well, whatever he had in mind, he sure sacrificed enough people for it. Everybody on the mission is dead except me."

"That could be one reason he doesn't want you to talk about it to anyone at the moment. Start rumors."

193

"What if I do, though?"

"Then we'd have to put a guard on you, restrict you to the villa, not let you go anywhere. So far you've been very good from all reports. You haven't tried to sneak off to Allied Headquarters or Naples."

"Yes, I've been good. I've obeyed orders and kept my mouth shut. But I can't do that forever. I'm only human. I saw terrible things done up North, Colonel, men die needlessly. And I think OSS was responsible for some of the suffering. Maybe not directly, but—"

"Well, my advice is to keep quiet until you've had a chance to talk to the general or somebody in Washington. Let them explain the situation to you. I know what you went through. I've read all the reports on what you told Major Nash in Como. Nothing seemed to work out right for your mission apparently."

"What if it wasn't supposed to?"

"What do you mean?"

"I'm not sure. But everything seemed to happen according to a plan. As if it came out wrong in the right way. Do you follow me?"

"Keep that to yourself. Now you'd better go back to the villa. It won't be long before you're out of here and on the way home. I envy you. It looks as if I'll be around for another six months even with the war in Europe over."

"It's not a bad life for you, is it, Colonel?" I couldn't resist saying.

"No, you're right, Sergeant," he said with a smile. "Not too bad."

I followed orders, and four days later I was sailing out of Naples on the *United States* with a couple of thousand combat troops. It was roomier and faster than the *Liberty Ship* I came over on that took two weeks in a convoy: five hundred guys crammed in a single closed cargo hold with one meal a day and the latrine at the head of the stairs overflowing every night. But at least then I did spend a lot of time on deck viewing the ocean and taking in the scenery—Gibraltar, the Atlas Mountains, the great white city of Algiers on the hillside. Now I spent most of the time five decks below, scarcely saw the ocean, and missed the passage through the Strait and the sight of the Spanish fishing villages.

Nobody else on board from OSS except a sergeant from the motor pool who stuck with me all the time and carried a .45. I asked him if he had orders to shoot if he heard me mention to anyone the mission I had been on behind the lines. He laughed, but not too convincingly, I thought. All he wanted to talk about were Italian women and American food. As for the war, it didn't exist for him anymore.

Just as I dreaded going overseas two years ago, now I anticipated going home. Yet the last night out, I began to dread that too for some reason. Instead of leaving the Pontiac mission behind, I was carrying it with me, and there would be no getting away from the people whom I had seen die. Not for a long time. No forgetting what I had done or tried to do and the ruins I had helped to create. Guilt and waste. Would they ever cease to haunt me? Up on deck I brooded out over the Atlantic. And probably the sergeant at my side saved me from drowning in my own pessimism, he and the singing and the excitement about who would see land first in the morning.

"I wonder," I said outloud to the wind and the waves and, I guess, to the sergeant too, "what it's going to feel like being back in the States, if it's going to be different than it was or the same old thing and what happened over there just a dream, the stuff you talk about years from now?" He didn't answer. He just turned and stared at me as if I were crazy, as if to say, "Aren't you glad to be going home?" And I could have been a little distracted at that moment gazing down at the ocean so dark, so deep, so close. Home never seemed farther off.

Chapter 19

As soon as we arrived at Hampton Roads, it was off the ship and on to Washington right away. No camp or even a delousing session. A jeep appeared at the dock and took us to the train. Then the long, slow ride north through Richmond getting reacquainted with the country—piney woods and mules going down sandy roads and main-street towns. There was a staff car waiting outside Union Station. And off we zoomed to Camp F in Maryland that the driver said was the Congressional Country Club. The city went by as fast as a bunch of postcards you thumb through in a drugstore—the Capitol, the Washington Monument, the White House. I even saw the Cabin John trolley I used to ride from the station up Pennsylvania Avenue to my room on F Street between 20th and 21st. Everything so unreal, so untouched by the war.

A bright warm Sunday afternoon. The pool and the lawn surrounding it were jammed. My first sight in over two years of tanned girls in bathing suits lolling on the grass exposing their backs and legs to the sun. People diving and swimming and a Glenn Miller record blaring through a loudspeaker. A disorienting spectacle that brought back so many wild, violent memories. And for a second I wondered what the hell I was doing in this strange place. Why wasn't I back in Dongo searching for the gold, stamping out the gold fever raging like a plague through northern Italy destroying everybody it touched? Even now standing before the huge clubhouse window gazing down at the swimmers and the sun-bathers, I could feel its eerie presence.

"Wow!" I said outloud to nobody in particular. "What a difference an ocean makes."

"You mean what a difference OSS makes," a tall, blond first lieutenant next to me said. "You'll get used to it. They all do."

But I didn't quite. For a week I slept in a tent with five other noncoms and had sessions with a psychologist in the morning and bowled and swam and played tennis in the afternoon. No KP. Movies every night, though no passes into town. The captain in charge wouldn't tell me whether I would be going back to the regular army, shipping out to the Far East, or staying with OSS in the States. And he didn't know about a scheduled debrief-ing of me by anybody at headquarters. So more isolation, more double-talk, more stalling.

And after a couple days of lolling around and living the good dull life, I didn't care what happened. Despite the green world and the luxurious clubhouse with its bowling alleys the place was beginning to resemble all the other reppo deppos I had been in from North Africa to Italy. Hours and hours of sitting around doing nothing but thinking about civilian life and cursing the army and the war, waiting for an order to send me somewhere to do something for some purpose.

Then it happened. One noon as I was finishing mess and planning to go back to the tent to sleep for an hour before a swim, an announcement came over the loud-speaker. Sergeant Del Greco was to report to the orderly room at two o'clock to go to headquarters in Washing-ton. Which meant taking a shower, putting on a clean khaki uniform and tie, shining my paratroop boots, combing my hair, pinning campaign ribbons to my chest. And reliving in my mind the whole Pontiac mission.

A captain was waiting at the orderly room with a

mustard-colored staff car and a chauffeur. A short, snub-nosed cheerful guy who reminded me of a trainer for a football team. He declared that he was taking me to see General Donovan.

At first the old excitement surged again, the same sort of feeling that I had experienced last winter as I climbed into the Flying Fortress at Maison Blanche outside Algiers for the flight to Lake Orta and the jump on Mount Mottarone. What an incredibly tense time that had been, the smooth flight across the Mediterranean, the anti-air-craft guns firing at us around Genoa, and the fires burning below in that ghostly snow dotted with black figures. But now that I had been there and come through suddenly I didn't want to talk any more about the melancholy mission and its casualties. I didn't want to know what lay behind it. All I wanted was to get out of this damn uniform and go back to school and become a lawyer, raise a family, live a decent life. No more wasting time on a war that when everything was said and done didn't concern me, at least not privately. Or I thought it didn't.

"You can sit in the back, Sergeant," the captain said, "since you're the VIP this trip." He and the driver got in front and we were off for the capital.

We drove to OSS headquarters at 25th and E Street, that shabby area above the Potomac with its coal yard and Negro tenements and rusty twin cylinders of the city's gas works. And I saw again the brewery with the green copper dome that always seemed so incongruous in the midst of the brick and limestone bureaucratic hives. Beer trucks loading while secretaries and professors scurried up and down the hill on the wooden walkway. Nothing had changed over the past couple of years, only more women, more cars, more officers.

"Look familiar to you?" the captain got out with me after we rode into the quadrangle and parked at the bottom of the wide steps leading up to A Building with its Greek pillars. Trees and shrubs filled the open space.

"Yeah, too familiar in a way. What do you think he wants to see me about?"

"I imagine he just wants a firsthand report of your mission. You were the only survivor, weren't you? He's a great one for debriefing guys who've been behind the lines and risked their necks. That's what this organization's all about, you know. At least to him. Sort of like a country editor who wants to hear about his reporters' experiences in person before they write them down. Don't worry, you have nothing to be scared of. Puts you at your ease in a minute. You'll never meet another one like him. A tremendous man."

"He ever call you in?"

"I never left Washington, Sergeant. I only trained you guys. They wouldn't let me go overseas. I tried to get assigned to a mission, but no dice. C'est la guerre."

The general did look tremendous all right, almost awesome to me, the stocky frame sort of pear-shaped, the ribbons brightening his khaki chest, the brigadier star on each shoulder, the sharp blue-gray eyes, the silver hair and ruddy Irish face. He greeted me at the door of his office, shaking hands, patting me on the back, calling me Vic. Inside, we sat alone amid maps, papers, books, and office furniture. A fan blew on us. And I thought, Christ, this is the man who was a close friend of Roosevelt!

"Well, Vic, you want to tell me all about it before I tell you all about it?" He laughed quietly.

"Yes, sir," I stammered, hesitating, fidgeting, not knowing where to look or how to begin. He offered me a cigarette, but I refused. Then finally I got going without quite meeting his gaze and recounted everything that had happened from the major's death at the Villa Carlotta to Bruna's appearance at my bedside in Como. He listened in a variety of moods, sometimes solemn, sometimes smiling, gasping and cursing, once even guffawing outright and once muttering, "Damn, we shouldn't have done that!" And when I finished exhausted, sweating, I felt as if I had been auditioning. For a couple of minutes, he didn't say a thing, sighing, reflecting, looking alternately at me and then off into space. I couldn't tell whether he was satisfied, disappointed, angry, or just plain bored.

"Now I'm going to tell you something, son," he moved closer with his chair, lowered his voice, "something that I don't want you to repeat for a long time, if ever. At least not while I'm alive. It's one of those wartime secrets that has to be forgotten." He paused. "I ordered Captain D'Alessandro to get that gold. He was recommended to me for the mission by Lucky Luciano through an intermediary. You know who he is, don't you?" I nodded. "He's in prison up in New York but has helped out our intelligence in several matters. I think in return for extradition to Italy after the war. The navy used him and his contacts during the Sicily and Salerno landings."

"You mean the captain wasn't a Communist, he didn't fight in Spain? He was Mafia?"

"No, he was in Spain all right and a Communist, a labor organizer in Macy's or Gimbel's. But before that he was a friend of Luciano. So were all of them, Carlo and Bruno, Donato and Silvio. Even the AMG officer in Milan, Rosselli."

"Christ, so you had the whole thing planned before Mussolini started on his flight to the Valtellina."

"That's right. We knew there was almost half a billion in his treasury and that the partisans or the Communists would try to take it, and the legitimate government of the country after the war might never see a penny."

"Was Major MacGregor's murder part of the plan?" I glanced at him.

"No, that was the terrible thing about it all. I told Bill to be careful, not to cross Mike. Keep tabs on him but stay out of his way. And I warned Mike no rough stuff. He could argue with Bill about Communism and arms drops, but that was it. I guess he felt he couldn't accomplish the mission without getting rid of him. Of course, Bill didn't know a damn thing about the plan to capture the Fascist gold. Nobody did except the ones I've mentioned."

"They doublecrossed you."

"They might have."

"About the capture of Mussolini too. Corvo had it all set up for us to take him at Como and then the major is killed and D'Alessandro takes over. Silvio is supposed to fly him from Bresso Airport outside of Milan to Caserta and he starts acting funny. OSS must have had a lot of plans to seize the guy."

"Yes, I think at one time we had something like twenty-five teams ready to parachute in and take him alive. But all of them got cancelled."

"You don't think they were deliberately sabotaged, do you, so the Communists could take credit for the execution of Il Duce? I mean they agree to give some of the Fascist treasury to D'Alessandro in return for his wrecking OSS plans to catch the dictator alive?"

"Yes, that could have happened. I just don't know. You see, son, you have to take all kinds of risks in this work, use all kinds of people, do anything to win the war. My God, we've got everything in this organization —movie stars, college professors, Wall Street lawyers, stunt men, bank robbers, business men, royalty, millionaires, writers, football players, college students, policemen, bums, politicians, labor leaders, philosophers, Communists, even a few prostitutes and priests. You name the profession or the trade and we've got somebody who fits the bill." He was silent for a moment, gazing past me with those keen blue eyes. "We might have had too many, and I might have lost control of them at times. But you have to admit we almost got our hands on that gold." He winked. "And it would have changed the political picture in northern Italy, possibly in the whole country. There'd be no strong Red

Party challenging the Christian Democrats. Maybe no Communist Party at all."

"So I messed things up for you. Is that what you're saying, sir? If I had left well enough alone, played along with D'Alessandro—"

"You might say you were a problem we hadn't foreseen."

"But they were going to smuggle the gold out of the country. They weren't going to give it to the Allies. It was strictly a Mafia operation, not a military one. And I could swear he made a deal with the Commies and then was doublecrossed after he doublecrossed you and them too. You ought to question Captain Silvio."

"Well, all that could be true. The main thing, though, is that no word of any of this must ever get out, especially our association with Luciano and my ordering D'Alessandro to seize the gold. It could be embarrassing for me, for OSS, for the government, for the President, and possibly downright harmful to you." Those blue eyes bore into me, smaller and sharper. "And don't forget I could be blamed for Bill's death."

"You mean you could be accused of ordering his murder to get the gold?"

"That's right."

"It was pretty brutal, worse than anything I saw, including the killing of Mussolini and the Fascists. Sometimes I think I'm going to have nightmares about it for the rest of my life."

"Are you the only witness living who saw him killed?"

"Yes, everybody else is dead or missing as far as I know."

"I realize your position, your feelings. These things can haunt you a hell of a long time. But you can't say a word to anyone, you understand? We've destroyed all papers and messages that might suggest there was such an operation involving the Fascist treasury, and that we had any connection with Luciano."

"No, sir, I won't say a word. I understand your concern. I just wish I knew when everything was happening what was going on and what D'Alessandro was up to. I still think he used you and then got used in return."

"Well, I want you to know how much I appreciate your work and your silence. From all reports I've read you almost got the gold for us single-handedly and stopped the execution of Mussolini. And really we didn't come out of the Italian campaign too badly. Dulles did a magnificent job handling the surrender with SS General Wolff. General Clark wired me the partisans we supplied were a great help in the final drive on the Gothic Line. This nasty little episode is best forgotten."

"I tried to do what I thought OSS wanted me to do on the Pontiac mission. But I'm wondering now if I had succeeded would I be alive today."

"Maybe not, Sergeant." He stood up and looked grave and then softened his expression. "Sorry there can't be any public recognition for you, no medals or letters of commendation. No mention in the official history of OSS either. As I said, we've erased the entire mission from the files. It'll be just as if the whole thing never happened."

"How will you account for the deaths?"

"German action against the partisans. I'm writing personal letters to the families of those involved. It's the least I can do under the circumstances."

"That's very thoughtful of you."

"Well, I was the one who initiated the mission. I feel responsible. It was just another one of those gambles we took that didn't quite pay off. One more thing, Sergeant." He lowered his voice, became extraordinarily confidential and paternal. "As I said, your life could still be in danger. Watch your step for a while when you get back to civilian life. That's where you're going in a couple of months in case you haven't heard. The war with Japan will be over then, once we reveal our secret weapon.''

I looked at him startled.

"Sorry, I can't tell you anything about it. But believe me, everything will be over by September. Now to return to what I was saying, be careful. They could still be out to get you.''

"Get me? Who?''

"The Communists and Luciano's men. Silvio and Rosselli are still alive, remember, and know about the operation. And Captain Donato and his two sergeants and Lieutenant Fusco haven't turned up yet. If you ever say a word about what happened or reveal anything of what I've been telling you, they wouldn't just deny it, they might dispose of you fast.''

"You mean I'm still expendable.''

"Afraid so. But don't worry too much about it. If you keep quiet, everything will turn out all right. Now goodbye and good luck, son.'' He shook my hand, patted me on the back and gave me that warm politician's smile before returning to his desk.

I walked out of the office toward the old guard slouching in the entranceway by the water cooler and the drooping American flag. Then through the portico with its gray Greek pillars and down the steps to the staff car waiting in the sun.

"Well, what did I tell you, Sergeant?'' the captain greeted me. "A great guy, huh?''

"Yes and no,'' I looked quickly at him. And as I got in beside the driver and gazed out at the massive buildings on every side, I couldn't help thinking what a waste, what a horrible waste, not just the war but everything it spawned from the bureaucracy and the obsessive secrecy to the dreams of empire and the achivements of power. And how relieved I felt to have come through and to know, at least what lay behind some of the horror. Or did I really know? Was the general telling me the truth about the Pontiac mission or only what he thought I suspected and wanted to hear? Was there

204

something else I would never know? He had leaked just enough to satisfy my curiosity and prevent me from ever talking about it again.

"You're silent, Sergeant," the captain called out from his big lonely back seat as we entered the grounds of the Congressional Country Club.

"I guess that's the way I'm going to be for a long time. OSS either makes you want to run out and tell your story to the nearest newspaper or bury it in the backyard like an old bone."

"And the general's persuaded you to bury it, right?"

"For the time being. I'll dig it up someday, though. Don't worry."

"I hope I live to read about it."

"Me, too," I turned around and smiled at him. "Me, too, Captain."

THE LAST NAZI
Max Lamb & Harry Sanford

PRICE: $2.25   T51486
CATEGORY: Novel

Canadian journalist Rod Baxter-Harrow returns to London from Israel after having written a sensational story about Adolf Eichmann. A scarfaced stranger in a London bar tells Rod a story that defies belief: hiding somewhere in Spain is Martin Bormann, Hitler's right-hand man and the cruelest Nazi of them all. Getting to Bormann would not be easy—especially since the most treacherous killers in Europe were hired to protect him. It was a tale the world needed to hear, if only Rod could survive to tell it!

HITLER'S LAST GAMBLE
Jacques Nobecourt

PRICE: $2.25 T51474
CATEGORY: War

Here, in full detail, is the true account of the most dangerous and dramatic battle of World War II— the Battle of the Bulge.

In December 1944—when she seemed on the verge of complete collapse, her armies driven from Normandy almost to the Rhine—Germany launched a sudden counter attack. The Battle of the Bulge was the last gasp of the Third Reich's great war machine and it proved to be the ultimate challenge to the strength and bravery of the U.S. Army.

NOW A BIG TV SPECIAL!

Murder In Amityville

Hans Holzer

PRICE: $2.50   T51408

MURDER IN AMITYVILLE
By Hans Holzer

This is the true story of Ronald DeFeo, Jr., now in prison for murdering 6 members of his immediate family in the house at Amityville, Long Island, where the next owners, the Lutz family, experienced the terrors depicted in "THE AMITYVILLE HORROR," the current best-selling book and movie.

Dr. Hans Holzer, renowned psychic investigator, who personally interviewed DeFeo in prison, reveals here for the first time the true story of DeFeo and others connected with this extraordinary case!